# Defenc ... s

## By

## Douglas Thornblom

# DEDICATION

I dedicate this novel to the fighting men and women of the United States Armed Forces, and especially to the men of the West Point class of 1966.

"A soldier is someone who, at some point in his life, wrote a blank check to the United States of America for any amount, up to and including his life."

# PROLOGUE

Saeed Mahmoudi, along with 12 other sun-browned men, sat quietly in a dark arroyo just south of the U.S. border and west of Ascension, Mexico, near the eastern edge of the Sonora desert. Unlike the other men around him, he was unafraid and patient, waiting for the signal from the "coyote" they'd hired to give the signal to move out.

He was an intelligent and educated man in his early 30's, called upon by his government to replace a critical coordinator who had the unfortunate luck of being killed two months ago in a common automobile accident. He was a good choice for a replacement. Mahmoudi was a Captain in the Iranian Quds Force, and he not only knew a lot about weapons, he also had experience in training Al Qaeda terrorists in Iraq on bomb making to use against U.S. soldiers. Some of his Al Qaeda trainees had later switched their allegiance to ISIS.

He didn't know the exact path that they would take to enter the U.S., but his informants and research had told him this particular "coyote," Miguel Martinez, was reliable and experienced. Thousands of men, women and children had made the crossing safely for many years now, and there was little price to pay even if caught, since the most likely outcome would be to simply return him back across the border.

He held a Sonoran driver's license and spoke a little Spanish as well as English, Arabic, and his native Farsi. But his Spanish was not so good as to fool a native speaker, so he isolated himself and kept his mumbled responses to questions simple and monosyllabic. This was not unusual behavior among the illegals waiting to cross over, as anonymity was a common concern, so he was generally left alone.

With a lot of patience and just a little luck, he would soon be across the border, and then he would quietly separate himself from the group. With the help of his GPS, he would navigate his way to the outskirts of Douglas, Arizona, where he would meet his contact for a ride northward.

His backpack contained several large water bottles, granola bars, dried fruit, energy drinks, two extra magazines loaded with 9 mm +P jacketed hollow point rounds, a lightweight rain jacket, and a miniature copy of the Koran. In his cargo pants waistline was concealed a Sig Sauer semi-auto pistol in a cross draw holster hidden under his loose, buttoned shirt. He didn't really expect to have to use a weapon, but he was ready if things went wrong.

It was early November of 2017, so hot weather wouldn't be much of a concern for him, but he was prepared for any and all circumstances. The gun and ammunition, as well as the Koran, could be quickly ditched if necessary. Although Mahmoudi hadn't been given a lot of time to prepare and travel to get to this point, Iran's overall schedule would soon be back on track. Any further delay would put a years-long, detailed plan at risk, just as it was nearing implementation.

But, he was smart and had memorized the key names, contacts and codes of his various regional leaders, who in turn would each alert their subordinate cell leaders, who would then contact individual teams to initiate the sequenced actions of a highly complex attack against the "Great Satan's" infrastructure. And, of course there were the hundreds of homegrown jihadists, that when publicly notified over certain websites that the massive jihad against America had begun, would take up arms, and join in the devastation.

Although Mahmoudi was not an Arab, he could count on a highly motivated cadre of devout Muslims of many organizations, from ISIS to Al Qaeda, all of whom had a common goal- that of destroying the United States as a world power, and bringing her citizens to their knees- especially after the shocking recent attack on his homeland. Sunnis and Shias have always been able to set aside their religious differences in the face of a common enemy. "The enemy of my enemy is my friend" in the Muslim world- at least temporarily, and under the right set of circumstances.

As he was pondering these thoughts, Miguel quietly passed the signal down the line to get ready. It was 1 a.m. and the small group began moving silently along the bottom of the arroyo, heading north, joining the 400,000 illegals that cross the U.S. borders or overstay their visas every year.

What Mahmoudi didn't know, because he had no need to, was that similar preparations had been made throughout Europe- and all attacks were coordinated to begin simultaneously in February of 2018.

# Chapter 1

Lieutenant Colonel (retired) Richard Cantrell and his wife, Sophia, had settled into their modest home in the Sea Breezes development, located on an island just off the coast of western Florida, near the growing city of Port Monroe.

The Cantrells had been fortunate to buy their one-story, 3-bedroom home in 2010, just after the disastrous decline of house prices, following the economic collapse of 2008; otherwise, they could never have afforded it. Fortunately, they had sold their northern Virginia home at a good price in 2007, before Richard's last tour in Afghanistan. But with his and Sophia's savings, including the profit from the sale of their Virginia home, they were able to put together a down payment, and with Sophia's salary and Richard's retirement pay, make the monthly mortgage payments.

Sophia was a middle school English teacher in Port Monroe, a position she was overqualified for, but was grateful to get, considering the poor economy. Richard had a difficult time finding a job- there were not a lot of opportunities for a retired Army Infantry Lieutenant Colonel in the existing economy, but he finally was able to find work as a part-time consultant to a security firm in Port Monroe. They both commuted across the new bridge to the island. The bridge was named for the now-deceased Florida state senator who played a leading role in making sure the bridge got funded, so the island could be developed as a bedroom community of Port Monroe. They struggled to make ends meet, but with careful spending and a strict budget, they managed, and were looking forward to their new life.

# Chapter 2

Richard Cantrell was born in San Antonio, Texas to a family of modest means, which meant he spent his high school summers working jobs, mostly in the lawn care business. He played high school football, but at 5'11" and 185 lbs. wasn't heavy enough to make first string lineman or fast enough to be a defensive or running back. But what he lacked in physical attributes, he made up with heart and drive, and he got his share of playing time. He loved sports, but football was his favorite, and he liked the camaraderie of having teammates that went through the grueling practices and games in the south Texas heat. He got elected to the student council his junior year, and was popular, especially among the teenage girls in his class. He was elected class president his senior year, and that, along with better than average grades and a good SAT score, got him admitted to Texas A&M, where he went through their excellent ROTC program, graduating in 1989.

He was an only child, so his parents were able to help him a little with his college expenses, and he worked in a Home Depot Lawn and Garden department during the summers to supplement what his parents couldn't afford. Upon graduation, he succeeded in getting a commission as an Infantry officer.

Sophia was a middle school English teacher in Port Monroe, a position she was overqualified for, but was grateful to get, considering the poor economy. Richard had a difficult time finding a job- there were not a lot of opportunities for a retired Army Infantry Lieutenant Colonel in the existing economy, but he finally was able to find work as a part-time consultant to a security firm in Port Monroe. They both commuted across the new bridge to the island. The bridge was named for the now-deceased Florida state senator who played a leading role in making sure the bridge got funded, so the island could be developed as a bedroom community of Port Monroe. They struggled to make ends meet, but with careful spending and a strict budget, they managed, and were looking forward to their new life.

## Chapter 2

Richard Cantrell was born in San Antonio, Texas to a family of modest means, which meant he spent his high school summers working jobs, mostly in the lawn care business. He played high school football, but at 5'11" and 185 lbs. wasn't heavy enough to make first string lineman or fast enough to be a defensive or running back. But what he lacked in physical attributes, he made up with heart and drive, and he got his share of playing time. He loved sports, but football was his favorite, and he liked the camaraderie of having teammates that went through the grueling practices and games in the south Texas heat. He got elected to the student council his junior year, and was popular, especially among the teenage girls in his class. He was elected class president his senior year, and that, along with better than average grades and a good SAT score, got him admitted to Texas A&M, where he went through their excellent ROTC program, graduating in 1989.

He was an only child, so his parents were able to help him a little with his college expenses, and he worked in a Home Depot Lawn and Garden department during the summers to supplement what his parents couldn't afford. Upon graduation, he succeeded in getting a commission as an Infantry officer.

During the Infantry Officers Basic Course at Fort Benning, Georgia, he had excelled enough to garner a slot in Airborne School, followed by the Army Ranger School. After getting his jump wings and Ranger tab, he was assigned to the 82nd Airborne Division and became a platoon leader. He was well-liked and respected by his soldiers, and proved himself to be a natural leader, never asking more of his men than he was willing to do himself.

He kept himself in top physical condition by running 3-5 miles every day after the long days of work, before heading back to his bachelor officers' quarters. In 1990 he deployed with his unit to Saudi Arabia for Operation Desert Storm, in what was to be his first of three combat tours.

His reputation and his outstanding Officer Efficiency Reports earned him an assignment to the 3d Battalion, 75th Ranger regiment, upon return from the war, where he rose through the ranks, and was selected as a Company Commander. After finishing his command, he was sent back to the 82nd, where he was promoted to Major and served as a Brigade Operations and Training Officer, or S-3. He was later selected for Command and General Staff College, followed by a trip back to Fort Bragg and the Special Operations Command.

After his return stateside from his tour in Iraq in 2004, he was driving to Savannah, Georgia, a town he had grown to love while assigned at Fort Stewart, for a little R&R. As he was driving south along I-95 a Toyota Celica a few hundred yards ahead of him started weaving back and forth, then slowed down and pulled off onto the side of the interstate with a blown out rear tire. He decided to stop and lend a hand, and when he pulled his Firebird behind the Celica and got out, he saw a leggy, dark-haired, shapely woman in a lightweight business suit step out of the car with a cellphone in her hand. As Richard pulled up behind her and got out of his car, she appraised the handsome man approaching her, and pocketed her cellphone.

Richard said, "Hi. Are you O.K.?"

"Thanks, I'm fine, just a little shook up.

"You handled the blowout very well, and kept control of your car. Looks like you could use a hand with that tire."

"Yes I'd appreciate it. I'm not really dressed for changing a tire." She held out her hand and said, "By the way, my name is Sophia."

      "I'm Richard. Pleased to meet you. Why don't you pop the trunk and I'll get your spare out. We can get you back on the road in about twenty minutes

It was a hot spring day, and Sophia was more than happy to have Richard give her a hand with the heavy lifting. Unfortunately her spare tire didn't have enough air in it, but Richard always kept an air pump and other roadside emergency equipment in the well of his Firebird for emergencies. After filling up the spare, he mounted it on the car's axle, tightened the wheel nuts, and put the flat tire in the trunk of the Celica. He was impressed that Sophia didn't mind taking off her suit jacket and getting her hands dirty along with him, and they both built up a sweat during the process.

The tire inflation and changing process gave them an opportunity to chat. It turned out that she worked as a school administrator in Savannah, and had lived there since graduating from college in 1993; and, she was also originally from Texas, so they had something in common to talk about while they worked. Their conversations slowed down the tire changing operation a bit, but neither seemed to mind. Sophia learned that among his friends, he preferred to be called Rich.

After the tire was changed, and Richard was getting ready to leave, Sophia turned to him and said, "Well, thank you very much for stopping to help me, Rich. I really do appreciate it. I don't think I could have done this by myself, not to mention that I didn't know I had an almost flat spare. In the future, I'll remember to check the spare when I check the other tires for pressure."

"No problem, Sophia, and you're welcome. I enjoyed talking to you."

After an awkward pause, just as Richard started to turn and walk back to his car, Sophia quickly added, "Then let me show you my appreciation by buying you a drink. If you're free this Friday, I get off of work around five and we could meet some place that we both know."

Richard was pleasantly surprised but recovered nicely and said, "I'd really like that. Just name the time and the place and I'll be there."

After running through a few possibilities they decided to meet at a Longhorn's restaurant that they both knew on the outskirts of Savannah at 5:30. They exchanged phone numbers then Richard headed back to his car and waited with his turn signal on until Sophia pulled out onto the highway. He followed her for a while to make sure the tire was OK, and as she signaled for her turnoff, Richard drove past her, caught her eye, and gave a little wave, which Sophia returned, along with a double beep of her horn.

Richard took a deep breath and said to himself, "Wow."

# Chapter 3

Sophia Koenig was born in the small town of Fredericksburg, in the Texas Hill Country. Growing up she was always tall and skinny, reaching 5'9" her junior year of high school. She was very athletic, and excelled in volleyball and basketball. During her senior year, she led her basketball team to the state finals, but injured her ankle during the fourth quarter and had to sit out a close but losing game.

But with her good grades and her basketball skills, she earned a small scholarship to Southwest Texas State University (which later shortened its name to Texas State University), which kept her in Texas and not far from her mother and her younger brother, Josh. Her father had died prematurely of a heart attack when she was in junior high, but he had had the good sense to buy a hefty life insurance policy that allowed the family to live comfortably and stay in their home. In 1990, when Josh graduated from high school, he joined the Marines and was off to Parris Island for his Basic Training and a career in the Marine Corps.

In college, Sophia was just an average basketball player, and barely succeeded in holding onto her scholarship. There was some family money left to help out, and she worked summer jobs in the local Wal-Mart and saved to help pay her tuition and expenses. She graduated with a degree in Education, and landed her first job in an inner city school in Savannah, Georgia that fall semester. She was no longer the skinny girl from high school; she had matured into a beautiful young woman.

After a little over four years of occasional dating, with no really serious relationship ensuing, she met a man a few years older than she, a graduate of New York University. His name was Alistair Yarborough, and he had recently arrived at her school from another Savannah district to serve as the new principal. Sophia was young, still a bit naive, and inordinately impressed with his self-confidence and grandiose manner of speaking. After accepting a date from him a few months after they met, they ended up in a relationship.

Under the circumstances, at the beginning of their relationship Sophia requested, and was granted, a transfer to a high school out in the suburbs, since she was essentially dating one of her bosses. Alistair opposed this sensible decision, which should have told Sophia something about him and raised a caution flag. They were engaged a proper six months later, and were married near his home in Boston after the 1998 school year ended. After a brief honeymoon in Martha's Vineyard, where Alistair seemed to spend more time with his old friends than with her, they returned to Savannah and their jobs.

## Chapter 3

Sophia Koenig was born in the small town of Fredericksburg, in the Texas Hill Country. Growing up she was always tall and skinny, reaching 5'9" her junior year of high school. She was very athletic, and excelled in volleyball and basketball. During her senior year, she led her basketball team to the state finals, but injured her ankle during the fourth quarter and had to sit out a close but losing game.

But with her good grades and her basketball skills, she earned a small scholarship to Southwest Texas State University (which later shortened its name to Texas State University), which kept her in Texas and not far from her mother and her younger brother, Josh. Her father had died prematurely of a heart attack when she was in junior high, but he had had the good sense to buy a hefty life insurance policy that allowed the family to live comfortably and stay in their home. In 1990, when Josh graduated from high school, he joined the Marines and was off to Parris Island for his Basic Training and a career in the Marine Corps.

In college, Sophia was just an average basketball player, and barely succeeded in holding onto her scholarship. There was some family money left to help out, and she worked summer jobs in the local Wal-Mart and saved to help pay her tuition and expenses. She graduated with a degree in Education, and landed her first job in an inner city school in Savannah, Georgia that fall semester. She was no longer the skinny girl from high school; she had matured into a beautiful young woman.

After a little over four years of occasional dating, with no really serious relationship ensuing, she met a man a few years older than she, a graduate of New York University. His name was Alistair Yarborough, and he had recently arrived at her school from another Savannah district to serve as the new principal. Sophia was young, still a bit naive, and inordinately impressed with his self-confidence and grandiose manner of speaking. After accepting a date from him a few months after they met, they ended up in a relationship.

Under the circumstances, at the beginning of their relationship Sophia requested, and was granted, a transfer to a high school out in the suburbs, since she was essentially dating one of her bosses. Alistair opposed this sensible decision, which should have told Sophia something about him and raised a caution flag. They were engaged a proper six months later, and were married near his home in Boston after the 1998 school year ended. After a brief honeymoon in Martha's Vineyard, where Alistair seemed to spend more time with his old friends than with her, they returned to Savannah and their jobs.

But Alistair slowly turned cold towards her, dedicating himself more and more to local and national Democrat politics during most of his free time. After the election of George W. Bush in 2000, and his rancor and depression over the fact, it soon became obvious that their personalities and their political differences were too far apart to be compatible. Sophia was a small town girl with conservative principles, and did not like her husband's bombastic and aggressive tirades in defense of liberal Democrat agendas. His cowardly comment in class regarding the attack on the Pentagon on September 11, 2001, that "at least one target was justified," pretty much sealed her opinion of him, and she filed for divorce shortly thereafter.

The divorce became final a few months later, and she moved into her own apartment. Her mother, who had never liked Alistair anyway, just said "Good riddance."

Rather than sit around feeling sorry for herself, Sophia began going to night, summer and weekend classes at Armstrong Atlantic State University in Savannah, and earned her Masters degree in Education Administration in just over a year and a half. Working and throwing herself into her studies didn't leave her much time for dating. She got her Master's degree in 2003, and the next school term got a job offer in a Savannah Middle School as the Assistant Principal.

Sophia had been the Assistant Principal at the school for just under a year when she met Richard on I-95. She had dated occasionally but found most of the men were too shallow, not very bright, or too aggressive for her tastes.

Richard, however, intrigued her. He came across as a polite gentleman, strong but not aggressive, and certainly handsome, and she found herself looking forward to Friday night.

She made a point of arriving early and sat in the waiting area with a bunch of papers in her lap. She had used the tactic before on first dates, to appear to have a lot of work to do in order to escape a date early, just in case Richard turned out to be like most of the other men she had met. After all, they had only talked to each other for less than an hour and she really had no idea who he was or what he was like. He arrived right on time at 5:30, greeted her with a nice smile and asked the hostess for a booth. After ordering glasses of wine, they sat and chatted over small things until the drinks arrived.

The conversation flowed naturally, and he actually listened to her and was eager to know her background. In turn, he honestly answered her questions about his Army service, without dwelling on himself. She was pleased when Richard suggested they stay for dinner, and she readily accepted his invitation. During their dinner conversation, she noted his intellect, as well as his strong build and dark brown eyes, and they lingered over their meal and coffee. Richard was charmed and smitten by this lovely woman. He asked for the check, and when it came, Sophia reached over and grabbed it and got out her credit card.

Richard protested immediately. "Wait, Sophia, I invited you to dinner."

Sophia smiled and said, "Yes, but now you have to ask me out again."

Richard was shocked, but he smiled back, and said, "OK, deal."

He walked her out to his car, and gave her a kiss on her cheek. They both knew that things were going to progress between them.

## Chapter 4

After that first night, they dated every weekend for a month, and found excuses to phone each other frequently. They ate out at restaurants, went dancing together, and spent a day at the beach. Sophia wore a modest bikini that took Richard's breath away every time he looked at her.

It didn't take long for Richard to realize he had fallen in love with this beautiful and intelligent woman, and he made a decision to commit himself. After dinner at her house one evening he asked her to spend Memorial Day weekend with him at one of Savannah's famed B&B's. This was a big step forward, as Sophia had been cautious and they had not yet been intimate. She accepted, both knowing that this was a big step forward as far as their relationship went.

Richard picked her up Saturday morning at her apartment. Sophia was wearing a pair of form-fitting jeans and a loose white blouse. Richard loaded her carryon into the trunk, and drove out to a lovely old inn near the river. After checking in, their elderly hostess took them upstairs to their room, gave a brief smile to Richard, and unlocked the door. She didn't bother with the usual room tour and description of amenities, she just handed Richard the key and said, "If you need anything, just ask, or if I'm not downstairs give me a call." She turned around and walked back down the stairs. Richard and Sophia walked in together and set down their overnight bags. Neither bothered to unpack.

Richard stepped up to Sophia and looked deeply into her eyes. They embraced, and kissed each other longingly. Richard took Sophia's lovely face in his hands, looked her in the eyes, and said, I love you, Sophia."

"I love you too, Rich. Very much."

Over the weekend, the new lovers spent every minute with each other, talking about their future, and dining in some of the excellent restaurants in town. Each evening they took short strolls down by the river, watching the reflected lights of the bars, shops and restaurants sparkle over the river's waters. Both were reluctant to leave Monday morning and return to their apartments, but they knew that this was the beginning of something special. Richard dropped Sophia off at her place, walked her to her door with her luggage, and kissed her.

"Sophia, thank you for a wonderful weekend. Let's do this again, soon."

Sophia gave him an enticing smile and said, a little out of breath, "We will, Rich. I promise." One month later, Richard moved in with her.

In July, they flew back to Texas to visit each other's families, and to announce their engagement. They were married in Savannah, surrounded by friends and family, in August of 2004.

Richard had orders for a staff job in the Pentagon, so Sophia had given notice to her school that she would be leaving her job and moving away. They bought their first house in northern Virginia that same month.

While at the Pentagon, Richard was promoted to Lieutenant Colonel and in 2007 was selected for battalion command and was assigned a battalion in Afghanistan. Since Richard was going to be gone for up to a year or more, they decided to sell their house so that Sophia could return to Fredericksburg and help take care of her ailing mother, who had recently suffered a minor stroke.

Josh Koenig, Sophia's brother, was still a Marine, now married with two children, a boy and a girl, and was stationed far away at Camp Pendleton in southern California, so they couldn't get away to help out for the months necessary for their mother to recover. Richard knew he would not be returning to the Pentagon, and since they didn't know where they would be stationed next, the decision for her to stay with her mother while he was overseas seemed logical. They sold their house at what turned out to be the top of the housing market and made a nice profit.

Richard picked her up Saturday morning at her apartment. Sophia was wearing a pair of form-fitting jeans and a loose white blouse. Richard loaded her carryon into the trunk, and drove out to a lovely old inn near the river. After checking in, their elderly hostess took them upstairs to their room, gave a brief smile to Richard, and unlocked the door. She didn't bother with the usual room tour and description of amenities, she just handed Richard the key and said, "If you need anything, just ask, or if I'm not downstairs give me a call." She turned around and walked back down the stairs. Richard and Sophia walked in together and set down their overnight bags. Neither bothered to unpack.

Richard stepped up to Sophia and looked deeply into her eyes. They embraced, and kissed each other longingly. Richard took Sophia's lovely face in his hands, looked her in the eyes, and said, I love you, Sophia."

"I love you too, Rich. Very much."

Over the weekend, the new lovers spent every minute with each other, talking about their future, and dining in some of the excellent restaurants in town. Each evening they took short strolls down by the river, watching the reflected lights of the bars, shops and restaurants sparkle over the river's waters. Both were reluctant to leave Monday morning and return to their apartments, but they knew that this was the beginning of something special. Richard dropped Sophia off at her place, walked her to her door with her luggage, and kissed her.

"Sophia, thank you for a wonderful weekend. Let's do this again, soon."

Sophia gave him an enticing smile and said, a little out of breath, "We will, Rich. I promise." One month later, Richard moved in with her.

In July, they flew back to Texas to visit each other's families, and to announce their engagement. They were married in Savannah, surrounded by friends and family, in August of 2004.

Richard had orders for a staff job in the Pentagon, so Sophia had given notice to her school that she would be leaving her job and moving away. They bought their first house in northern Virginia that same month.

While at the Pentagon, Richard was promoted to Lieutenant Colonel and in 2007 was selected for battalion command and was assigned a battalion in Afghanistan. Since Richard was going to be gone for up to a year or more, they decided to sell their house so that Sophia could return to Fredericksburg and help take care of her ailing mother, who had recently suffered a minor stroke.

Josh Koenig, Sophia's brother, was still a Marine, now married with two children, a boy and a girl, and was stationed far away at Camp Pendleton in southern California, so they couldn't get away to help out for the months necessary for their mother to recover. Richard knew he would not be returning to the Pentagon, and since they didn't know where they would be stationed next, the decision for her to stay with her mother while he was overseas seemed logical. They sold their house at what turned out to be the top of the housing market and made a nice profit.

Fate has a way of intervening with life's plans, however, and only four months after Richard arrived in Afghanistan, his battalion was ordered to send two of his companies to establish outposts in an area near the base of the Hindu Kush mountains, with a mission to clear out a Taliban force that had been intimidating the local villages. Their follow-on mission was to provide security for the larger villages, establish friendly relations with the local tribal and village chiefs, and help out the villagers, with such projects as medical and dental civic action programs, and eventually USAID food assistance. Richard's men were also assigned to arm and train fighters in the local villages that were opposed to the Taliban.

Richard made occasional trips via helicopter to the outposts to check on his men, and to meet with some of the village leaders, but on one of his visits, things went to hell in a hand basket. A small team of Taliban fighters armed with AK-47's and RPG's had been waiting on the high ground near the last landing zone (LZ), and when Richard's Blackhawk took off they opened fire. He had always ensured that he varied the routes and times of his trip, but it was almost as if the terrorists had expected his arrival, which was not an uncommon occurrence in Afghanistan. The Taliban maintained a web of informants throughout the country, especially around the headquarters of major units and airbases from which U.S. forces operated.

Thankfully, the RPG's fired at his chopper missed- since the RPG is a line of sight weapon, it is a lot harder to hit a moving aircraft at distance, although at closer ranges several helicopters had been shot down by RPG's. But the AK fire hit the aircraft on Richard's side, and he caught two of the rounds. Although wounded herself, the pilot managed to keep her damaged aircraft in the air, flying low for several kilometers to distance them from the withering fire before she had to set it down hard. The copilot was on the radio during the short flight giving a situation report, their location, and requesting a medevac.

Of the two bullets that hit Richard, one hit his left thigh and shattered his femur, and another penetrated his side, perforating his stomach. Some piece of jagged metal, probably from the helicopter's skin, also tore a deep gash across his left cheek near the side of his mouth up to his temple, barely missing his eye. Richard's radio operator was unhurt, and as soon as the Blackhawk hit the ground, he dragged his boss out and quickly patched up Richard's major wounds with their field dressings as best he could to stop the profuse bleeding. The copilot assisted the pilot and bandaged her wounds, while two other soldiers, one of them Richard's Sergeant Major, set up quick security positions on either side of the downed bird.

Richard had lost consciousness, and was medevac'd, along with the copilot, back to Kabul where he underwent emergency surgery. The docs and nurses there did a good job of patching him up and keeping him alive, but he needed more advanced surgery than they could give him. After Richard was stabilized, he was medevac'd again, this time back to Walter Reed Army hospital, near Washington, D.C., where more surgery was performed.

Sophia was notified the next day and was sick with worry. As soon as she found out the details from the Army, she flew up and met Richard at Walter Reed and stayed with him for the several months of his rehabilitation. Her mother had already recovered sufficiently from the effects of her stroke to live on her own, so Sophia rented an apartment near the hospital so she could be with Richard as much as possible.

Richard worked hard at his physical therapy, lovingly assisted by Sophia, and with her help and encouragement, made a remarkable recovery; however, he would certainly never jump from an aircraft again, and he would walk with a slight limp for the rest of his life. Richard thought the scar on his cheek was unsightly, but Sophia smilingly chided him saying that he didn't know much about women, as she considered his scar rugged and manly, adding to his good looks.

After Richard's recovery, much to his disappointment, he was assigned again as a staff officer at the Pentagon. But Richard was not a desk jockey type of soldier. If he couldn't be with troops, he didn't want to ride a desk shuffling papers for the rest of his career. After a long discussion with Sophia, in June of 2010 he submitted his retirement papers. With 21 years of service, and having served the minimum of 20 years needed to qualify for retirement, he received a much-deserved but modest pension. At the age of 43, Richard and his 39-year-old wife set out on a new phase of their lives.

Sophia gave notice to her school that she would not be returning for the next year, and they spent a few final weeks in their Fairfax, Virginia apartment doing research on places to retire. After giving their priorities a great deal of thought, they decided that they would first look for a nice place they both wanted to live, with finding jobs a necessary, but secondary, consideration. Richard reasoned that after living in tents and sleeping bags for so many years in the Army, if he had to, he could live in a trailer with Sophia and be happy; Sophia was not quite as sanguine about that idea, but she understood what Richard was saying and went along with the general sentiment.

# Chapter 5

Richard and Sophia had originally assumed they would retire in Texas, but they both had always wanted to live near a decent beach, and unfortunately, Texas didn't have many of them, at least that they could afford to live near. And, Richard had just about had his fill of hot, dry weather during his tours in the Middle East anyway. Beachfront property was of course out of the question, but after spending a lot of time online they narrowed down several beach communities in Florida that were not only attractive, but because of the huge drop in Florida house prices during the recession, affordable, as long as they stayed well away from the expensive beachfront developments. Also, Florida was one of the states that did not have a state income tax, and Floridians generally looked very favorably on the military, both of which were big pluses for a military retiree.

They took their 3-year-old Toyota Highlander, loaded it up with important papers and memorabilia that they didn't want to entrust to movers, and headed south to check out several areas their research showed as promising. They also turned the trip into a semi-vacation, taking time to explore the beaches and local towns along the Florida coasts. They stopped first in Jacksonville Beach, then St. Augustine, and continued down the coast to a few other cities on the Atlantic. Several of the Atlantic coast towns were out of their price range, but Jacksonville Beach was at the head of their list, until they got to Port Monroe on the west coast.

The Port Monroe area, and particularly a new community called Sea Breezes on Phelps Island, jumped to first place on their list, especially when Sophia got an offer for a teaching job in Port Monroe that would be available in the fall. Sea Breezes was a middle class community in the narrow northern part of the island, and was especially hard hit by the housing recession. Sales of homes had stopped, and many homes were foreclosed on over the next year or so. Both the developer and many homeowners were victims of bad timing.

Almost 20 homes were for sale when they arrived, and several lots were empty and overgrown, or had only framework completed. After some hard negotiation with the distressed developer, and an offer to put down 20% on one of the smaller houses, their offer was accepted, and a local bank agreed to the loan, based on Richard's secure Army pension and Sophia's job acceptance. Richard and Sophia signed the papers and moved in, and Sophia began teaching in the fall of 2010. A few months later, Richard finally got a part time job with a security company in Port Monroe.

# Chapter 6

Port Monroe, on the west coast of Florida, was named after President Monroe, who in 1821 signed a treaty with the Spanish for control of Florida, for the princely sum of $5 million. The port city was located on the Gulf of Mexico, at the mouth of the Naranjos River, which for many decades had served as an important route of commerce from the western coast to south and central Florida. Port Monroe was founded on the site of an old Apalachee village, and thanks to a natural deep-water port, and some judicious investment by the state in the early 20th century, had grown to become a small but successful port for commercial shipping for western Florida.

The island that was off the west coast of the city was named Phelps Island, but whoever Phelps had been, and why the island was named for him, was lost to history. Prior to the construction of the connecting bridge to the mainland, Phelps Island had only one small fishing village on the gulf coast near the center of the island, and a few dirt roads and small hunting cabins in the wooded areas.

In Florida, there were large tracts of unoccupied land, including many coastal islands, that had previously been considered uneconomical for development, until an ever-expanding population, especially of retirees moving down from the North, made formerly inaccessible land now economically viable to develop. Helped along with some generous contributions by developers to the right city and state politicians to lift restrictions and provide funding for the infrastructure needed for new communities, things began to change over the last few decades.

Phelps Island is a relatively small island, stretching from southeast to north and shaped more or less like a pear, with the top oriented to the north. The center of the island, what would be the fat part of a pear, was just off the coast of the north side of Port Monroe. Like most Florida islands, the terrain was relatively flat, with no peaks and just a few small hills and cliffs on the southeastern side, and mostly flat lands on the north. Along the northern shores there were forests, ending in saltwater marshes. There were a few natural ponds on the island, but no creeks.

The distance from the island to the shore had made the island uneconomical to develop for decades, since the only way to get there was by boat. But the housing boom that started in the early 2000's made the prospect of developing Phelps Island feasible. The growing population of Port Monroe, along with political lobbying, convinced state lawmakers to allocate money to build a two-lane bridge out to the island to open it up for development.

The bridge project was completed in 2004, and named for a recently deceased politician who had led the fight for the bridge. It had a drawbridge that allowed small ships and boats to pass, but since the bridge was on the northern side of the Port Monroe, which was mostly warehouses and housing developments, and away from the main port to the south, not much traffic passed through.

The island's widest point, essentially the base of the pear-shaped island, measured barely three miles, and its length was about four miles from top to bottom. The northern end was just one mile wide.

Phelps Island also offered some protection for the port and city from the periodic tropical storms and hurricanes, and in 2014 a small oil refinery was built on the north side of the port, adding some much-needed jobs to the area. After the construction of the bridge, the small fishing village and cabins gradually disappeared as developers came in and bought land for housing developments and shopping centers. The first and most profitable development was a gated beachfront community, called Sunset Beach Estates, which was developed on the gulf side of the island, with 36 expensive homes and two condos, along a half-mile of the island's only one mile or so of decent beach.

Fortunately, the newly incorporated City of Phelps Island had designated the rest as a public beach, and had the foresight to set up parking areas for Port Monroe and Phelps Island beachgoers. Shops and restaurants naturally followed, as did individual homes scattered throughout the island.

After the most profitable development on the beach was begun, another upscale community along the southeast side of the island was started. This next development consisted of 52 houses and several high-rise condos, in another gated community called Pelican's Landing, encompassing most of the area of what would be the bottom of the pear-shaped island. There were no beaches here, but from the hills and cliffs, there were some nice views of the waters of the Gulf of Mexico. The far, narrow northern part of the island remained undeveloped for several years.

In 2006, the last development that was begun was Sea Breezes, consisting originally of Phase I, with 86 houses, and plans for adding a Phase II to the north. Phase II was to have two entrances, one through Phase I, and another entrance off a road along the east side of Phase I, which never got beyond being a construction access road. These two large plots of land were at the northernmost end of the island, with several hundred yards of woods on three sides, which acted as a buffer to the marshland beyond. Sea Breezes was located to the north of the road that led from the bridge to the Phelps Island beach (uninspiringly but appropriately named Beach Parkway).

The Sea Breezes development was bound on the south by shopping centers, gas stations, and small stores that were built off the north side of the Parkway for easy access, and it was bound on the north by a track of land that was originally intended to become a 66-home Sea Breezes Phase II.

But the recession killed the Phase II plan, and the developer wound up filing for bankruptcy in early 2012. The land remained cleared but undeveloped, except for a few partially built homes, and would be tied up for almost two more years in bankruptcy and tax courts. That was the situation in Phelps Island when the Cantrells moved in.

# Chapter 7

Unlike so many developments in Florida, Sea Breezes was actually built with some forethought in mind. Work had begun in 2006, at a time when houses were still selling almost as fast as they could be built. The developer laid out an unusual but very practical construction plan. One of the exits off of Beach Parkway to the north passed through the shopping areas and on northward into Sea Breezes. The four-lane road was called Sea Breezes Drive, from which the development took its name. As you entered the community, there were houses along both sides of the entrance road, which then split into a circle, around a man-made lake in the center, before continuing on into what would have been Phase II.

The lake was oblong-shaped and roughly 160 yards in length and 110 yards wide. Instead of building homes that backed up to the lake, as was done in almost all other communities, the developer had left a little grassy land around the lake, planted it with oak trees, then fenced it all in with an attractive 6-foot high black aluminum fence, with decorative spiked points along the top. They added a few picnic benches and covered barbecue pits and tables on one side, and an enclosed playground on the other. All Sea Breezes residents were issued a key to both gates, for the picnic area and the playground, so that every homeowner in the community could enjoy the lake views.

Sea Breezes was a deed-restricted community with a Home Owners Association, HOA, and strict bylaws that stated in no uncertain terms that children under 18 were not allowed in the lake area unless accompanied by an adult parent or guardian, and no one was allowed after dark without special permission, for events such as birthdays and parties.

Infractions were dealt with by imposing heavy fines, and after a few $500 violations, the residents learned to respect the rules, or more accurately, make sure their teenage children did. Sea Breezes was designed to be a middle class community, so no money was spent on a community pool, which kept down the annual HOA dues.

Off of Sea Breezes Drive, and Sea Breezes Circle, that went around the lake, were several short streets ending in cull de sacs along which other, more modest houses were built. All of the streets were named for historical figures of Florida history, such as Monroe, Jackson, and Flagler. Of course, the most expensive and largest houses were on Sea Breezes Circle around the lake. The shorter, winding streets made optimal use of the remaining land so the developer could create as many lots as possible. Sea Breezes Drive ended at a northern gate that would be the entrance for Sea Breezes Phase II. There was also a 6-foot high sturdy vinyl privacy fence around the entire Sea Breezes Phase I community.

Richard and Sophia Cantrell's house was located at the end one of the cul-de-sacs, on Monroe Drive. They had neighbors to their left and right, and their back yard was against the vinyl community fence, on the other side of which was the vacant land to the north that would have been Phase II. Because of Richard's leg wounds, they had opted for a one-story home in order to avoid him having to go up and down stairs. Besides, the one-story homes were smaller and cheaper.

# Chapter 8

The Cantrells really enjoyed their new home and the new community. Most of their neighbors were friendly, and they were an eclectic mix of retirees and young professionals, with many of the retirees originally from northern states that had come down to Florida to escape high taxes, and enjoy the lower cost of living and the warmer climate.

Sophia enjoyed her teaching, but Richard was still struggling with getting used to only working irregularly in a part-time job and was looking for something else to do to bring in more, and a more steady, income. He spent a lot of his time working on their yard and maintaining their house, and since he had a lot of free time, he also did a lot of studying online to learn about investments, now that the markets had begun to recover.

Less than a year after they had moved in, Sophia's mom had a massive stroke in her home when she got up one summer morning. Fortunately, it was later determined that she had died almost immediately, as no one found her until the next day, when a neighbor friend came over to find out why she wasn't answering her telephone.

Sophia and Richard immediately hopped a plane to Austin, drove to Fredericksburg, and met up with Josh and his family there to help settle the estate. Sophia's mom had lived frugally and still had substantial savings that had held up through the market crash, as she didn't trust the stock market and had kept her money invested in CD's, rolling them over as they came due, and living mostly off the interest. Her will left her estate divided equally between Josh and Sophia, and after selling the house, car, furniture, and other possessions and cashing in the CD's, both of her children ended up with roughly $290,000 each- a sad but unexpected windfall.

While the two siblings were dealing with the myriad details of handling their mother's estate, the two families spent a lot of time together, and had plenty to talk about. After 22 years of service, Josh had reached the rank of Gunnery Sergeant in the Marine Corps, and like Richard, had served three tours over in the "sand box" of Afghanistan and Iraq. His wife, Carmen, was not happy with the frequent separations, and neither were their two children, who missed their dad when he was gone from home so long and so often. To make matters worse, Josh would be up for reassignment next year, and there was a real possibility he would end up in Afghanistan again, if not this assignment then certainly the next one.

# Chapter 9

Carmen and Josh had met during one of his assignments at Parris Island. She was a Carolina gal, from a large immigrant Cuban family. She began selling real estate after she finished junior college, and kept doing so after her marriage to Josh. Over the years she had earned decent money, although it was difficult having to start over in a new location every time they moved. But she had a wonderful and outgoing personality, and her dark Latina good looks didn't hurt her in getting quickly established, and selling houses, in each new location; that is, until the children arrived, and then she had to cut back on work a lot to raise her family. But they had been able to save some money over the years, and with the new windfall from the inheritance, retirement was all of a sudden a distinct possibility.

After returning to California, Josh and Carmen had some long discussions about their future, and they finally decided that Josh would retire. The main motivator was the possibility of Josh being sent back to Afghanistan again, so he put in his retirement papers right away, and was informed that his retirement date would come in just three months. Carmen and Josh then started the same process that Richard and Sophia had gone through in trying to decide where to go, whether to Texas or South Carolina, and what kind of job Josh would look for. But during Josh's retirement leave, they decided on a visit to Florida to see Sophia and Richard, and talk to them about how they had navigated the retirement process. It proved to be providential.

Neither really could say at the time whether or not they had in the back of their minds all along the idea of moving to Sea Breezes and being near Richard and Sophia, but that's the way it turned out. They had taken the family once to Florida for a short visit with them the first Christmas after the Cantrells had moved in, and the whole Koenig family liked the community and the nearby beach. House prices in the summer of 2011 were still pretty low in the area, and at the end of their visit, they ended up buying a small four-bedroom, two-story house near the community entrance. No one could accuse Josh and Carmen of being indecisive. They moved in as soon as they left California, and Sophia and Richard helped them get settled in.

Carmen got hired right away by the local office of a national real estate chain, but Josh's job prospects were no better than Richard's. The kids were used to moving to new towns, and they settled in quickly and made new friends. Anita, the youngest, was 13 years old and her brother, Sean, was 15. Both were energetic and outgoing kids, but well behaved, and good students- about what you'd expect of the children of a Marine "Gunny" Sergeant.

Two months after their move-in, on an evening after getting the kids off to bed, Josh and Carmen poured some brandy and relaxed in a comfortable discussion of their circumstances. Josh was frustrated, and couldn't see any job for himself on the horizon in the slow economy. Carmen understood his frustration, and after a lot of back and forth, Carmen floated a proposal. They discussed the pros and cons and they reached an agreement.

Josh would set up a home office and handle all the administrative and financial details of Carmen's real estate agent job, as well as take care of the kids after school and on weekends, which allowed Carmen to work full time. This plan not only freed up Carmen for more selling time, but it also took care of the need to hire an after school caregiver for the kids in her absence. Josh saw the logic in this, but grumbled about being a "kept man," much to Carmen's amusement.

But the Koenigs' announcement of their decision at the next family get-together at the Koenigs' house hit home for the Cantrells also, and when they got back home, Sophia floated the idea of Richard quitting his part time job and concentrating on his interest in financial planning and investments, since now they actually had some money to invest. The only thing they had done with the inherited money was to sell Richard's old beater that he used to commute to and from work, and buy a new Subaru Outback.

They decided that Richard would quit his part-time job and start investing, at least initially just for himself and Sophia, but probably later for his own folks, still living in San Antonio. Once the Koenigs found out about the Cantrell's decision, Carmen and Josh asked if Richard would do some investing for them also, and offered to pay him a 1% commission, since neither of the Koenigs had any experience in investing in the markets. Richard agreed to manage their investments, but steadfastly refused to take any payment for his work. Since Richard no longer needed a car for work, Sophia got the Outback and Richard inherited the old reliable Highlander that brought them to Florida.

Of course, Josh also good-naturedly chided him for becoming a "kept man" like himself. But the next morning, Richard set about making up an investment strategy for the Koenigs and opened a brokerage account for them.

# Chapter 10

Richard came up with diversified portfolios for both families' investments, consisting of a mix of technology stock ETF's, an S&P 500 ETF, and for balance, an intermediate bond fund. He didn't trade, he just left the investments alone, figuring that the ups and downs of the stock market were actually indicating a long-term rise due to the Federal Reserve policy of keeping interest rates at zero in the hopes of stimulating a weak economic recovery from the recession.

Both Richard and Josh had contemplated contributing to the work of the Sea Breezes Home Owners Association, but after attending a few meetings, they both became disgusted with the petty politics and personal power plays of the HOA's board members, most of whom had little organizational experience and were striving to gain some personal status and authority that they had never enjoyed in their careers. The guys figured it would be best if they let the petty political machinations of the squabbling board members vying for status and power take care of themselves, and just make sure they obeyed the community bylaws.

The Cantrells and Koenigs understood that too much family too often was not a good thing, so they got together only once a month or so for dinner, drinks, or outings to the beach. This approach worked out well for everyone, so that when they did get together, it was special and not tedious.

Richard and Sophia enjoyed their additional time together, and had a very rich and satisfying life. They both made efforts to stay healthy and in shape for each other, and had set aside three days a week for late afternoon workouts at a new gym that opened up on the island, in order to keep their weight under control and keep their bodies in shape.

It didn't seem possible that Sophia could actually enhance her drop-dead gorgeous looks now that she was in her 40's, but Richard swore she got more beautiful with each passing year. Richard's wounded leg limited his workouts- no more running, which had been his lifelong passion before being wounded- but he made up for that by spending extra time on the recumbent bike at the gym, which allowed for vigorous lower body workouts without the harmful impact of running, or weight-bearing step machines. Although his hair was now salt and pepper, his muscled upper body and relatively flat stomach (he had put on about 10 extra pounds since his Army days) attested to his dedication to staying in shape.

Being that three of the four adults were from Texas, and the men both having served careers in the armed forces, among the common interests the two families shared were shooting rifles and pistols at a local indoor/outdoor range in Port Monroe. Although both of the men had hunted in their youth and early careers, they no longer had any interest in going hunting. They preferred instead occasional family outings for an afternoon of target and skeet shooting, and the guys taught the Koenigs' kids, Anita and Sean, to shoot pistols, rifles and shotguns. Richard and Sophia had both gotten their concealed carry permits shortly after arriving in Florida, and Carmen and Josh did the same after they moved in.

After the Koenig children went to bed, the adults had discussions on a wide variety of topics, including the state of the United States' politics and foreign policy. None of them was happy with the way the recent and current administrations were leading the nation, and they were disappointed to watch the United States cede its role as a world power. They were all particularly concerned about the rise of Islamic terrorism and the unimpeded expansionist dictatorships in China and Russia seizing ever more power and influence throughout the world.

After the reelection of Barack Obama in 2012, they all expected that things would get worse as far as national security was concerned, and they decided it would be prudent to stock up a little more on some additional weapons and ammunition, as well as some freeze dried food, first aid supplies, water purification devices, etc. After the tragic events of the theater shooting in Colorado and the school shooting in Connecticut, they watched as anti-gun lobbies used those events to push for legislation to tighten control over, or outright ban, many types of weapons and magazines, complete with some states banning or mandating registration of certain weapons, in clear violation of the 2nd Amendment. But no one organization or political party had the clout to oppose the juggernaut of restrictions, so all the restrictive laws stood. Fortunately, not all state and municipal governments succumbed to knee-jerk reactions to give in to the anti-gun lobbies' agenda, and fortunately Florida was one of many states that did not.

Richard was an accomplished online shopper and found good deals not only on weapons, ammunition and survival food, but also on good, large safes to store the weapons and ammo. Josh and he both bought stand-up safes to secure their modest stockpiles, making sure to bolt them into the foundation of their home office closets with extra long steel lag bolts drilled into the concrete foundation. Richard had noted that in 2012, some snowbird residents of the beachfront community of Sunrise Beach Estates had their valuables stolen by thieves during their extended absences. Rather than trying to crack the safes, they simply drove up to the homes in moving vans and loaded the safes onto a truck and drove away, allowing them to crack them or cut them open at their leisure and without risk. No one would be doing that with the Cantrells' and the Koenigs' safes.

Richard and Josh made sure to time their purchases in between tragic shooting events, immediately after which prices soared and ammunition became both scarce and expensive. Both men understood the nature of the current Federal firearm regulation watchdogs, and accumulated their ammunition, and particularly their weapons, over a period of several years so as not to attract attention and get on any Federal watch lists.

Neither Josh nor Richard considered themselves "preppers"- they had no cabin in the woods or underground bunkers, no "bug out" plans, and neither had any interest in or ties to right-wing so-called militias. They simply wanted to be prepared to stick out a temporary catastrophe with their families in place, never really thinking that the United States would come under an "end of the world as we know it" type situation. They actually both believed the most likely use of their supplies would be due to a hurricane strike that knocked out power and commerce for weeks, as Hurricane Katrina had done in 2005, along with the accompanying vandalism and shootings. Neither had any idea how wrong their assumptions would become.

By the spring of 2015, the investments Richard had made had almost doubled, and he started slowly selling most of them, taking profits for both of the families. He believed that since the markets had gone almost straight up for six years, there was bound to be a major correction at some point, so once it was thought that the Federal Reserve would begin raising interest rates, he moved most of his money into investment grade individual corporate and municipal bonds, with the intention of holding them until maturity. He no longer cared if the stock market went up or down, as long as the companies whose bonds he held didn't go bankrupt, which was highly unlikely. Since both gold and silver prices were down, he converted $5,000 of each of the families' cash into silver and small denomination gold coins, which they stored in their safes.

# Chapter 11

In that same spring of 2015, Richard and Sophia were having dinner at home one evening, and after they had cleaned up the dishes Richard brought up a subject he had wanted to discuss for months.

"Honey, there's something I've been thinking about and I'd like to float an idea by you. I've been putting it off for a while because we've been so busy, but I thought that maybe we might consider getting a dog to keep me company at home. Since you're gone every day, I'm here alone and it would be nice to have a companion."

Sophia smiled as he was saying this and said, "You know, Rich, we always had a dog when Josh and I were growing up, but I just really hadn't thought seriously about it until we settled down here. I've been thinking about us getting a dog some day too, so since we both want to, let's just do it."

Richard grinned, leaned over and gave her a kiss, and said, "I'll start looking tomorrow. Did you have any particular type of dog in mind?"

"Well, I don't want one of those little yappy dogs, but I don't want a Rottweiler either. Why don't we check the Port Monroe dog pound, or whatever they call it, and see what they have? Maybe we'll get some ideas."

The next Saturday morning Richard made some calls, and after lunch, they drove across the bridge to the Port Monroe Humane Society.

As the entered the kennels with a young woman named Taylor, one of the volunteers on the staff, they found over a dozen cages with dogs in them, many of which started immediately barking up a storm. There was one cage with a small mongrel dog and her puppies, as well as several older dogs. As they went from cage to cage, their hearts went out to the animals, because some of them were either too old or injured to ever be adopted. Some even growled and snapped, and there were ones that had been abandoned and had gone feral. There was little hope for those dogs either.

As they were walking around, Richard noticed a medium-sized dog in a shoddy-looking cage near the back entrance. He went over and saw an exceptionally furry dog, a female, that was obviously mostly Siberian Husky, but had some other mix in her also that he couldn't identify. As he looked into the cage, the dog eyed him warily, but neither barked nor growled. He noticed how skinny she was, and also noted her thick black and white coat and beautifully shaped face. He was surprised to see the dog looking straight into his eyes, seemingly appraising him also, and it was then that he noticed that she had one blue eye and one brown eye. He asked Taylor what her story was.

Taylor said, "Actually, she was dropped off at our front door the night before last, and we didn't have any other cages immediately available, so we cleaned up the one she was brought in, until we can move her into one of our cages. We've only just checked her out, but she seems fairly healthy, but malnourished, and she was obviously abused because she is very hand shy. It looks like she's also been in some fights with other dogs, as she has some scars near her neck, flanks, and on one ear. They don't look too bad, so she must have defended herself pretty well. Maybe you guys will take one of the dogs and make room for her in a regular cage."

Richard called over to Sophia, and said, "Honey, come over here, I want you to look at this one."

Sophia came over and looked at the dog and the first thing she said was, "Rich, she looks awfully skinny." Turning to Taylor, she asked, "What kind is she?"

"Well, we're not sure- definitely mostly Husky, and maybe some Shepard or even Wolf. You'd have to run a genetic test to find out for sure."

Richard asked her, "Would it be all right if I opened the cage and tried to pet her?"

"Sure, go ahead, but be careful. We haven't had her try to bite any of us yet, but she's very defensive, and she may growl a little."

Richard had had dogs when he was growing up also, so he knew how best to approach a strange dog. He looked at her and talked to her soothingly as he reached his hand in down low with his palm down. "Hi there, girl, is it OK if I pet you?"

The dog shied away, but didn't growl. She eventually sniffed Richard's hand a bit, and after a few moments allowed him to rub his hand under her chin as he kept up a dialogue of "Good girl, good dog," and other soothing chatter. He then slowly moved his hand to the top of her head, and stroked it back toward her perked-up ears. The dog never made a sound, but didn't shy away either, and Richard figured that was enough for a first encounter.

Sophia repeated the process and got the same results, only as she was withdrawing her hand she got a quick lick from the dog. She smiled at this, turned to Richard and said, "Well, what do you think? She's a little bigger than I was thinking of, but I think she's got a lot of potential."

Richard looked at Sophia, noticed the expectant look on her face, grinned and said, "Let's take her."

After going through all the paperwork and paying for her shots and other fees, Richard picked up the cage and put it in the back of their old Highlander. It wasn't heavy, as the dog weighed only 36 pounds. As he left he handed Taylor an additional $50 donation for the Humane Society, thanked her for her help, and he and Sophia got in the car and drove home.

On arriving home, Richard carried the cage out to their fenced-in back yard, set the cage down on their back patio, and opened the cage door. The dog just sat there looking at him without moving. Sophia went inside and got a bowl of water and put it just outside the cage... still no movement. They both decided to go back into the house and just watch her from one of the windows.

After a few minutes the dog cautiously crept out of the cage and quickly looked around, obviously wary of danger. After being satisfied that no one or thing was around to hurt her, she walked up to the bowl and lapped thirstily at the water until it was almost all gone. She then went out to the grass and peed and came back to the cage, entered it and lay down facing out.

After about 20 minutes, she repeated the process of creeping out of the cage and looking around, then walked a few yards over to a big maple tree, and lay down in its shade, keeping her wary eyes moving around, watching the door and the back gate on the community fence that Richard had installed.

Richard and Sophia looked out the window to check on her periodically, and then Richard went in to the fridge, got out a hot dog, and cut it into bite-sized chunks. He put the dish in the microwave to warm it up, took the dish and opened the door, then slowly approached the dog. The dog stood up and her hackles went up as Richard approached, but using the same soothing voice he used back at the humane society, said, "Hey, girl, are you hungry?" The dog sniffed the air, but didn't move, so he knelt down and put a couple of pieces of hot dog down at the edge of the patio and backed away.

The dog slowly got up and with one eye on Richard stepped over and quickly gobbled up the treats. She looked up at Richard expectantly, obviously very hungry, and he sat down on the patio and tossed another couple of pieces out between him and the dog. She approached closer, and when Richard stretched out his hand and offered her the remaining pieces, she slowly came closer and lapped them up from his hand.

Richard turned around and said to Sophia through the open back door, "Hon, I think we'd better go shopping for some dog food."

Not only did they get dog food, they came back with a carload of other things- a collar and leash, a dog bed cushion, chew sticks, food and water bowls, a rubber ball, and a rope pull-toy. On their way back home, Richard asked Sophia, "Well, have you thought about any names for her yet? We can't keep referring to her as 'the dog' forever, and we've got to call her something."

"Yes I have. She's mostly Siberian so I thought we'd give her a Russian name."

Richard thought a minute and said, "OK, that sounds like a good idea, did you have one in mind?"

Sophia quickly said, "Yes. How about Natasha?"

## Chapter 12

By the summer of 2015, the Koenigs and the Cantrells had settled into comfortable lives that had allowed them to take annual vacations back to Texas to see friends and family, and the Cantrells had even booked a two-week tour of Europe. They had both been to Europe before, but not together, and they settled on a tour of several European capitals for June of 2015.

When the Cantrells left for Europe, they left Natasha with the Koenigs, which delighted the kids, as they loved playing with her in their back yard. By then, Natasha was used to the Koenig family after several visits to each other's homes. She had settled down and put on weight, so they had no qualms about leaving her with them while they were gone.

During the Cantrells' tour of Europe, they were shocked to see the state of affairs in the countries they visited. On their first stop in England, the tour group saw so many Muslims in the capital that one of their fellow travelers referred to the city as "Londinistan." As they traveled on to Paris, Madrid, Rome, and Athens, they noticed that these cities also had a lot of Muslims, many of them poor North African refugees. They harbored no ill feelings towards these people, since most were refugees only looking to escape the brutal violence of war-torn Africa and the Middle East- but they were everywhere, either begging on street corners, or on side streets with wares laid out on old blankets to sell. Both of the Cantrells felt sorry for them, and even bought a few things from them at the asked-for prices instead of bargaining with them.

But the truth is that Europe's welfare economies and union-mandated labor laws insured that some governments were burdened with ever more crushing debt. Unemployment was high, especially among the younger population, which stubbornly remained above 20%, and over 40% in nearly bankrupt Greece. Overcrowding, crime, and civil unrest, not to mention continuing and ever-bolder Islamic terrorist attacks had begun to make travel to Europe not only disconcerting but also dangerous.

The open borders policies of the European Union that allowed hundreds of thousands of unscreened Syrian and and other Middle Eastern Muslims to stream in from war-torn Syria and its surrounding nations would get far worse later in the year, and some of the overflow would reach the United States, with devastating consequences. When the Cantrells read of the horrific Islamic terrorist attacks in Paris in November of 2015, a massacre that killed and wounded hundreds of Parisians, and was perpetrated by at least two of the recently arrived Syrian refugees, the Cantrells decided they would not risk travel to Europe again.

The United States had some of the same problems that Europe was now encountering, and for the same reasons, but not on the scale of Europe- at least not yet. The thousands of new Muslim immigrants only added to the tens of thousands of Muslim immigrants already admitted over the previous decade. Many of these joined with, or helped radicalized, homegrown Islamic extremists. It was only a matter of time before a critical mass would be reached.

Adding to the immigration problem was the fact that the U.S. economy was still stagnant, the massive government debt continued to pile up, and the cost of social welfare and other unearned "entitlements," all led to less money for national defense, and meant even further reductions in the Armed Forces. Many of Richard and Josh's military friends had been forced into early retirement, and the younger officers and NCOs they had served with were simply dismissed via so called Reductions in Force, some without compensation because they had fallen short of the 20 years minimum of service required to earn a pension.

With the United States failing to take any lead in addressing the wars in Syria and Iraq, and against ISIS in general, by late 2016 the Middle East had slid unchecked into anarchy and violence. Iraq had ceased to function as a viable state, and was disintegrating into tribal and religious factions and fiefdoms, with the Shiite areas virtually ruled by Iran. ISIS had already taken over most of Syria, in spite of Russian intervention on behalf of Assad, as well as large parts of Iraq and Lebanon. Afghanistan, Libya, Sudan, and Yemen had almost ceased to exist as functioning nations, falling into constant warfare among rival factions and tribes.

Attempts to curtail Iran's nuclear weapon ambitions via various treaties and agreements had failed miserably, with international inspectors being denied into sensitive military nuclear sites, frustrating the inspectors, but surprising no one but the idealistic and gullible politicians of the West. The Iranians had nothing to fear, as there were no longer either the means or the will to enforce agreements among the Western nations.

But Israel was another matter.

# Chapter 13

The recent feckless, hands-off government policies in the Western world's approach to the Middle East had not gone unnoticed by the Israelis. Europe has had a centuries-old history of anti-Semitism, ranging from the expulsion of Jews from Spain by the Catholic Kings in 1492, to the pogroms of Eastern Europe, to the Nazi extermination camps. European anti-Semitism extends to modern times, albeit a little more subtly, although most Europeans would deny this.

Israelis learned shortly after its founding as a nation that the only ally it could count on to stem world anti-Semitism was the United States. But that changed dramatically beginning in 2009, and by 2016 it was painfully obvious that Israel could count on only limited, and often just meaningless rhetorical support from the U.S. And even that limited support was waning.

Israeli Prime Ministers had for years watched as the West pretended to isolate Iran and prevent the Ayatollahs from getting their hands on a nuclear weapon, while leaving huge loopholes in sanctions, and ignoring repeated violations of various international agreements and sanctions. The Israelis had one of the world's premier intelligence agencies, combined with an ability to reach out and strike at its Muslim enemies. The Muslim world had a great fear of the Mossad, and with reason. In previous years, Israel had succeeded in tearing apart Iranian centrifuges with their Stuxnet software virus, not to mention infiltrating and recruiting operatives to assassinate Iranian nuclear scientists known to be working on Iran's nuclear weapons program. But that was becoming ever more difficult to do without the cooperation of the United States.

In spite of assurances by the U.S.'s politically influenced intelligence agencies that Iran was not able to build a nuclear weapon, Israel knew better. U.S. intelligence agencies, along with so many other Federal agencies, had learned to toe the line of the Obama administration's international political agendas.

The Israeli Air Force had been denied the most sophisticated technology available in the warplanes they bought from the U.S., but that didn't stop their scientists from upgrading their capabilities themselves. Not even the U.S. knew how much they had been able to accomplish in this area, and Israel no longer trusted the U.S. to share this information.

In the spring of 2017, the Israeli Prime Minister had used one of his regularly scheduled cabinet meetings to discuss an extremely important and risky plan of action. Security was normally very tight at these meetings, but attendees noted an unprecedented level of security surrounding this one. The Prime Minister struck off all other items on the official agenda to discuss the very difficult decision on whether or not to conduct a massive air strike against Iranian nuclear facilities. The chiefs of various Israeli intelligence and diplomatic agencies were in attendance to present the latest intelligence and political situations.

There was no doubt that Iran was within months of developing a small nuclear weapon, if they hadn't already obtained one by purchasing one from North Korea, Pakistan, or Russia, and although the weapon in question might not be able to be fired from a missile yet, it could easily be smuggled anywhere in the world via international commerce networks, using false flags and doctored cargo lists.

The evidence was compelling and on a close vote, the decision was made to launch a preemptive airstrike to take out, or at least heavily denigrate, Iran's primary nuclear weapons facilities. Everyone knew that this would be costly, and there was no way they could even mention their decision to the U.S., much less count on any support for a strike. Remembering the treachery of the Yom Kippur war, in which a coalition of Muslim countries invaded Israel on their holiest of days, the Prime Minister proposed a strike date of June 25, 2017- the last day of the Muslim holy days of Ramadan.

There was more than a symbolic reason for this date. Arabs around the world would have just finished a month of daylight fasting and would be celebrating the end of the holidays- a good time for an attack, when the Iranian armed forces would be at their weakest and least prepared.

Over the years the Israeli Defense Force, the IDF, and the Israeli Air Force in particular, had held mock exercises simulating such an attack, so they had become commonplace for intelligence agencies to note. The next one would not be an exercise.

There were three possible routes from Israel to the nuclear sites in Iran. One would take it on a circular path skirting the border of Syria, another would be a direct shot over Iraq, and a third would be over Saudi Arabia airspace. Although Israel's diplomatic and intelligence agencies thought Saudi Arabia, a sworn enemy of Iran, might look the other way, the feeling was that they could not count on that benign acquiescence. The Israeli Air Force, or IAF, did have 11 air refueling tankers based on the Boeing 707 airframe, but distance and flight time was still a factor. Since Iraq was no longer a viable entity, the planners decided on the quickest route, a direct flight from Israel to Iran.

The IAF held no illusions on the difficulty of this mission. Many planes would be shot down; some would not have sufficient fuel to return home, even if they survived Iran's Russian-supplied S-300 advanced air defense missiles; still others would be shot down by a few surviving, hastily-launched Iranian Air Force fighters. The pilots knew that this was a do or die mission, perhaps a Masada moment for the IAF. But they were determined to get the job done, and hopefully destroy Iran's nuclear capabilities, or at least degrade it for years to come.

Israel had the ability to launch nuclear warheads capable of reaching Iran, as an additional backup in case of total failure by the IAF, but only as a last-ditch resort. Israel also had a small fleet of Dolphin-class diesel submarines. Getting them through the Straits of Hormuz into accurate striking range of Iran would be just as difficult, if not more so, than getting warplanes into Iran proper so they could bomb their targets. But Israel was prepared to take losses here also in order to get within striking range of the Dolphins' cruise missiles. These submarines could also be armed with nuclear tipped cruise missiles, and although Israel did not want to use them, they would be employed if the conventional strike failed. Simply put, failure in this mission was not an option. The Israelis knew full well that as soon as Iran got its hands on a nuclear weapon, their country would be destroyed- a powerful motivator for all the brave warriors concerned.

# Chapter 14

Unlike the U.S., with its modern, politically correct penchant for passive names for military operations, such as "Provide Comfort," "Inherent Resolve" and "Restore Hope," the Israelis were more militant and direct. The upcoming attack on Iran was code-named a more martial sounding "Operation Lightning Bolt," and was launched just after midnight Israel time on Sunday, June 25, 2017.

In Washington, D.C. most of the government workers were still at home for the weekend and the president was on a fund-raising mission to big donors in California. It was early morning in Tehran at launch time and the Israeli attack planes would be arriving over Iran as dawn approached, to begin their final attack runs.

The air attack went not nearly as well as hoped but not quite as bad as feared. Over 96% of the aircraft launched got near the eastern border of Iraq, but once in range of the new Russian-supplied air defense missiles, a disheartening 26% of the original aircraft were lost close to or over the Iranian border. Before the first bombs were dropped, Israel had already lost almost a third of its attack force. Of course, IAF planners had expected a large loss, and had designated primary and secondary backups to all targets.

All the planned targets were hit, with almost a 70% success against the most important nuclear facilities. But the IAF had planned for more than just the destruction of the nuclear facilities- the elite Iranian Revolutionary Guards bases were also targeted, as well as oil refineries and power plants. The intent was to avoid killing Iranian civilians as much as possible, and great care was taken to minimize that. But the Israelis knew that they also had to degrade Iran's ability to retaliate for a long time to come.

In the final analysis, Israel paid a horrendous price. Another 34% of the original strike force was lost during the bombing, and with refueling problems, damage, and other causes on the return flight, only 36% of the original assault aircraft landed at Israeli air bases. Only a small number of the downed pilots were rescued by helicopters, almost all on Iraqi soil, and some of the downed pilots in Iraq were captured, tortured, and slaughtered by various Iraqi or Islamic terrorist factions.

Just over a third of the heroic pilots and aircrews eventually returned home- but the mission was accomplished. In all, the casualty rate of the attacking pilots in the strike force was 59%. Again, not as bad as had been feared, but not as good as had been hoped.

The Israeli submarine force never got the chance to become involved in the attack. The first sub to enter the straights of Hormuz on June 23 was detected by U.S. naval forces, and its detection was unfortunately announced publicly by the U.S. administration. Israel pleaded that the sub was merely on an operational exercise, and the sub quickly withdrew, along with the other submarines deployed miles behind it that were ready to follow.

The Israeli cabinet was outraged over this betrayal, but in the interest of concealing the impending attack, the Prime Minister made public apologies to all for its ill-advised "exercise." Nevertheless, the Israelis attributed many of their losses to the slightly enhanced security posture that this caused the Iranian armed forces to adopt.

# Chapter 15

The IDF had called up all reserves the day of the attack in one of the many call-up exercises they had conducted over the years- but this time it was for real. Units deployed all along the border, and flooded the Israeli Arab neighborhoods with police and soldiers, with orders to shoot anyone threatening violence. A 6 p.m. to 6 a.m. curfew was also imposed.

Army units along the borders engaged outraged Palestinians and Arab and Iranian-backed terrorist organizations such as Hamas and Hezbollah, hastily attacking Israel territory, and reserve soldiers guarding neighborhoods used lethal force against violent attacks by Palestinians. Many car bombs and suicide attacks were successful, but the Israeli security forces had expected and planned for this, and succeeded in thwarting most of them before too much damage was done.

Fortunately, all these attacks were uncoordinated, overall largely ineffective, and eventually suppressed. The Israeli Prime Minister issued a no-nonsense warning to Iran, the Muslim world, and anyone else so inclined, publicly admitting for the first time that Israel did in fact have a significant nuclear arsenal, and that any invasion of Israeli territory by any nation, or its surrogates, would be met with a nuclear response against their capitals. This was one "red line" that was both believed and respected.

Predictably, the international outrage, from Europe to China, was immediate and ferocious. U.N. resolutions were made to condemn Israel and to cut off all commerce with the Jewish nation, but the U.S. administration, faced with a successful fait accompli, and finally some support of Israel by American Jewish organizations, reluctantly vetoed the measures.

Iran was not in any position now to retaliate after the devastation of the Israeli attack, although they stepped up their threats to wipe the "Little Satan" from the globe, as well as increasing their "Death to America" rhetoric. But they had good reasons not to react at this time, since they already had a long-standing operation in place against the "Great Satan" and the West. The attack by Israel, and the veto of the U.N. resolutions by the U.S. only reinforced their plans to destroy America; in fact, they contacted their Chinese and Russian allies to get some technical help in augmenting their attack plans, and to speed up the timetable.

Now all they needed to do was hunker down, repair their infrastructure, and wait for their plan to build up and unfold. Patience was one of the Muslim world's greatest virtues over the Western nations, and they knew their time was soon approaching for revenge.

# Chapter 16

Saeed Mahmoudi had easily made it to the large Muslim enclave in Patterson, New Jersey during the busy Christmas holidays of 2017. He had plenty of time to establish himself in a small apartment previously rented for him by one of his local operatives, who would also participate in the initial attack. He stocked it with food and supplies, and began to contact his regional leaders across the U.S., using innocuous code words, to let them know that he was in place, and that everything was on track for the final plan. He kept a very low profile, not even attending services at the local mosque, feigning a serious, chronic illness to his neighbors that kept him almost housebound.

In late January, Mahmoudi alerted his regional leaders that implementation of the first phase of the attacks was imminent, and to make sure that they did not all react until he gave them the appropriate signal to implement the countrywide second phase attacks to be followed a few weeks after. He did not give a specific date for the second phase of attacks for security reasons.

The first strike was designed as a psychological attack that was both tactical and strategic. On Mahmoudi's command to his selected local jihadists, at 9:30 a.m., the four main automobile river tunnels in the New York City area were collapsed by massive truck bombs loaded with the same type of homemade fertilizer-based explosive that was used in the Oklahoma City bombing back in 1995. All of the explosions were coordinated, and occurred within eight minutes of each other, during rush hour on the cold first Monday morning of the 5th of February, 2018.

The loss of life was horrific. Markets that had just opened crashed, and the New York Stock Exchange quickly closed, just as they had after the 9/11 attacks. In typical "closing the barn door after the horses escaped" fashion, all government entities raised their security alert status to the highest level. The president appeared on national TV to issue the standard declaration that the backers of the perpetrators of the heinous attacks would be "hunted down and prosecuted." Congressional investigations were promised.

Of course, immediately after the attacks the press went wild with 24/7 coverage and endless analyses, with talking heads nodding sagely that this was obviously the work of a local terrorist group of unidentified origin, and although tragic, since there were no further attacks over the next few days, "increased awareness" should continue. But after a week or so of no further attacks, and with politicians such as the mayor of New York City assuring everyone that the terrorist attack was a one-off event, the media proclaimed that here was no need to continue heightened security. As after the 9/11 attacks, the stock markets reopened in a few days, and life gradually returned to normal.

Mahmoudi knew the Americans well, and let the American public relax as the government returned to the normal loose security of American cities and facilities. There were no leads or clues to be analyzed, as both the trucks and the jihadists who drove them, were blown to bits, and lying at the bottom of the Hudson and East Rivers. The government had wound down the alert in time for the long President's Day weekend, and many of the security personnel involved took time off from a lot of overtime work for a much needed rest.

## Chapter 17

Richard was at his computer reviewing the stock market data at the 9:30 opening when the markets plunged to their daily limit maximum and were halted. His bond holdings had actually increased in value before trading was halted in the bond market minutes later. Something bad had happened and he turned on the TV and heard about the attacks on New York City's tunnels. All channels had the same coverage- it was like 9/11 all over again. Sophia was already in school so he called Josh. "Josh, turn on your TV."

"What's going on?"

"Looks like some kind of attack on New York. I'm going to call Sophia and you'd better call Carmen, and get them home as soon as they can, just in case.

"Jesus, look at that," Josh said, watching reports of the devastation of the tunnels in New York on TV. "OK, talk to you later."

Richard dialed Sophia's cell phone. She always insisted that her students turn off their cellphones in class, and she always did the same, so he had to leave her a message. By the time she returned his call at the lunch break, the news had already hit the school. It was decided that school would remain open unless there were further attacks. She called him back during her first class break and they decided to just wait and see what happened.

Richard called Josh back and they discussed the situation. Richard said, "Josh, just to be on the safe side, why don't we head down to the grocery store and stock up on some food and supplies, just in case."

They agreed and headed to the local Publix grocery store. There were others there buying a lot of things like canned food, bottled water, candles, etc., but the crowds were orderly and patient. In addition to the above items, Josh and Richard also added plenty of dried fruit and packaged preserved meats, including lots of Josh's favorite snack, Slim Jims; actually, he cleaned the shelf of them. On the way home, they filled up both cars with gas. Richard reminded Josh that both families had better make sure they always had at least a half tank of gas in their cars at all times.

After their wives got home they all met at the Koenig's house for dinner and a discussion of the day's events. There were no further attacks, so they concluded this was another 9/11 type attack. Josh said, "I hope they are able to find out who was responsible and if it was a state-sponsored terrorist group, hit them back hard." But as the days went by, no one claimed responsibility, and nothing happened, so life went back to normal in the United States, and in Sea Breezes - until February 19th.

# Chapter 18

At 1 a.m. on Sunday morning, the 18th of February, in the middle of the President's Day long weekend, Saeed Mahmoudi set in motion via coded messages over the internet, calls over "burner" cell phones, and encrypted emails to his regional commanders, an order that initiated the chain of notifications, down to the lowest jihadist, to launch the all-out attacks. At dawn, many of the country's major bridges, power plants, including nuclear plants, major ports, oil refineries, pipelines, and government buildings, were attacked, in nearly every state, coast to coast, throughout the day. The devastation was horrendous.

Iran had long had large stockpiles of various types of radioactive material, including U-238 and some of the radioactive isotopes used in medicine, such as Cobalt and Cesium. ISIS and Al Qaeda had also been able to buy radioactive material on the black market, from Russian-supported former KBG thugs and criminals given access to supplies recovered from some of the former Soviet Union states, especially Moldova.

Long before the Israelis attacked Iran's nuclear facilities, small quantities of highly radioactive elements had been carefully smuggled into the the U.S. by jihadists traveling through similar routes that Mahmoudi had traveled, plus the less watched areas of the Canadian border. After more than eight years of successful smuggling, there was enough material to make nine "dirty" bombs, combined with large quantities of explosives for maximum dispersal of the highly radioactive material. On the 18th of February, dirty bombs were detonated in some of America's most strategic cities: Washington D.C., New York City, Los Angeles, Chicago, Miami, San Francisco, and Houston. Two more were reserved for Fort Bragg, North Carolina and Fort Hood, Texas. Although immediate casualties were not that extensive, the radiation that was dispersed ensured that parts of these cities and forts would be contaminated for years or even decades. The radioactive material did not spread as it would in even a small nuclear weapon detonation, and there was little to fear of radioactive contamination outside of the cities affected, but once reported, mass panic occurred in all large cities and military bases across the U.S., and mass exoduses followed.

Not all of the jihadists' pre-planned attacks were successful. Some of the operatives were on intelligence watch lists due to carelessness and were intercepted and killed or captured as they attempted to execute their attacks. But while security officials dealt with the major attacks, the homegrown jihadists followed on later in the day, as planned, with smaller attacks that lasted for several days, against population concentrations such as apartment buildings, hotels, and airports, where stranded passengers were bedded down waiting for some miracle to get them home. These attacks were made primarily with small arms, firebombs, and the occasional home made improvised explosives.

Even more of these untrained terrorists were stopped by authorities and by vigilant local police. But all of the terrorists who survived the initial attacks carried on with additional attacks, most of them willing to die for Allah. In the post-attack confusion, some were successful three or even four times before being killed or captured.

Simultaneously with the initial physical attacks, Iran, with the help of their Chinese and Russian allies, unleashed massive cyber attacks on American infrastructure and financial institutions, shutting down power grids, air traffic control networks and banks, as well as some of the government's most critical communications systems, including the FEMA national radio system. Planes were not dropping out of the sky, but many were lost trying to land at the nearest airports in bad weather, their pilots without any radio communication or navigation aids, but determined to get on the ground as quickly as possible, fearing there might be bombs on their planes.

Regular and National Guard Army units were called up to help secure damaged and remaining government installations, in an attempt to prevent further attacks. But the reality of the situation was that many of those soldiers, especially the National Guard and Reserve troops who had regular jobs and lived in towns instead of on more secure military bases, simply did not show up during that long weekend. This was because they were either away for the long weekend, or lived off base and their first priorities were taking care of the immediate security of their own families. By the time units were semi-organized enough to deploy, the vast majority of the damage had been done and there were few terrorists left to fight. These units, along with regular Army units, were deployed to help maintain law and order, but they could not be everywhere, and they also had to be rotated so individual soldiers could look after the well-being of their own families as the days dragged on.

The devastation was such that travel, commerce, financial markets, and almost all U.S. economic and government activities were shut down. By the end of the second day, America was in shambles, with most of the nation without power. Air, rail, and sea transportation was almost completely non-existent. With banks closed and ATMs powerless, there was no functioning monetary system. It wouldn't be too much longer before currency was of no use anyway.

Saeed Mahmoudi had given the signal to launch the final attacks, but he was no simple-minded martyr. He remained in place, with plenty of food and water stashed away. He knew that any soft Western society was only nine missed meals away from anarchy.

# Chapter 19

Richard had never been cured of his military habit of waking at the crack of dawn, and he had just fixed his early morning coffee on the chilly Saturday morning of the 18th of February, and turned on the TV. What he heard and saw was astonishing. He called Josh and said, "It's happened again, only a lot more serious, and all over the country, with some cities reporting radioactive contamination. Grab some cash and gold coins out of your safe, wake Carmen, and let's take all four cars to Publix, now! Don't wait on us. We'll meet you over there."

He woke Sophia, almost pulling her out of bed, and helped her get dressed as he told her the news, and hurried her to her car. They took off to the Publix, which opened at 6 a.m. every morning, and this time there was a crowd. They loaded up baskets of food but by the time they got to their turn at the casher, the young girl told them that the credit card system was down and she could accept cash only. They paid, and noticed the Koenigs a few registers over doing the same. Some people left their carts, and others just said to hell with paying, and pushed their carts out the door while employees stood helplessly by, shouting at them to stop. The store manager took out his cell phone and dialed 911.

The situation was degenerating quickly. Both families took their cars back, dumped their loads in the garage, and headed back to Publix for a second time. But by the time they got there the store had closed its doors, and police were trying to control an increasingly desperate mob. Gunshots were fired, and the Cantrells and Koenigs decided to get the hell out of there. All four adults had their carry weapons but they had no desire to get into a shootout, as looters started breaking the store's windows.

All four cars then headed over to the nearest gas station and filled their tanks. Then Josh had an idea, and hollered over to Richard and Sophia, "Let's head over to the 7/11."

The 7/11 was tucked away in a small strip shopping center, and was just a few blocks away. As they pulled up, the owner was getting ready to close up shop. Leroy Ivory had no TV in the store, but a previous customer had told him there had been some kind of terrorist attacks against the United States. He asked Josh if he had any details of what had happened, so Josh filled him in.

Leroy was a good guy, a Black man with short silver hair and a quick smile. He and Josh had become friendly, both having served in the Marines. Like Josh, Leroy had also retired as a Gunnery Sergeant, but his war had been in Vietnam.

Josh explained to Leroy about the widespread attacks, and asked him if he would let them shop for some things if they paid him with gold coins. They each offered him five 1/10 oz. pure gold American Eagle coins, if they could fill up their cars. Leroy said, "OK," went up to the front of his store, closed the door and flipped the sign over to read CLOSED. The four of them started loading up their cars out back. When Richard returned for a few more items, a couple of rednecks in a pickup drove up and started banging on the door. One of them had a jack handle in his hand. Richard drew his gun and pointed it at the first man and said, "This store is closed. We're here to provide security, so go way." Looking down the barrel of Richard's Bursa Thunder Pro 9 mm semi-auto, both of the young thugs backed away quickly and drove off looking for an easier target.

Richard turned to Leroy and said, "Leroy, you'd better pile everything you can into your car and head home. Things are getting ugly, and they're only going to get worse. There are already riots in the Publix shopping center, and a lot of people are going to have the same idea those rednecks had, and show up here. We'll stay and protect you while you load up your pickup, but we all need to leave quickly. I'll guard the front while Josh stays with you out back, and the ladies can help you load." Leroy gulped, nodded, and did what Richard suggested.

Leroy told them he would take his load of food home and then come back and protect the store. Josh asked him if he had more adult family members with guns, and he said no-there were just he and his wife, and the only gun he had was an old Mossberg 500 12-gauge shotgun he kept at home. Josh shook his head and advised him not to return to the store.

"Listen, Leroy, what you have left isn't worth dying for. Here, take my old Marine .45 pistol, you know how to use it, and this extra magazine. Go home and tell your wife what has happened, and plan on hunkering down for a while. Don't worry about the gun- I have others, and when this is all over you can give it back to me. No one knows just how bad this is going to get or how long it's going to last." And then the lights went out.

They all drove away and headed back to their homes, where they unloaded the food and started putting things away. As the Cantrells were pulling into their driveway, they heard a tremendous explosion and felt a shock wave that rocked their car. The refinery on the mainland, near the southeastern tip of the island, had been blown up by terrorists, and the explosion was so massive, it destroyed or damaged dozens of warehouses and businesses around the refinery, as well as nearby homes on the mainland and even on Phelps Island. The situation on the southern part of Phelps Island was worsened when an oil tanker that was anchored offshore caught fire and blew up, flattening or burning dozens of homes in Pelican's Landing, and damaging the Phelps Island bridge.

As they ran into their house, they tried to call the Koenigs on the phone but the line was dead, and there was no service on their cell phones. Sophia looked at Richard with tears in her eyes. Richard wrapped his arms around her and hugged he tight as she wept- they both knew then that their situation was going to continue to deteriorate, and they feared that this was all going to end up very badly.

# Chapter 20

Although Josh and Richard were not "preppers" they had taken some precautions, mainly in case of a Katrina-like situation due to a hurricane strike, a very common occurrence on the Florida gulf coast. Both families now took inventory of their supplies and weapons on hand.

Richard and Sophia had two pistols each, an AR-15 5.56 mm rifle, and a semi-auto shotgun, in addition to several thousand rounds of ammunition. Josh had been a hunter, and had several hunting rifles plus a DPMS Panther 5.56 mm carbine, and several pistols that he had collected over the years. He also had .22 pistols and rifles for his kids.

With several dozen cans of freeze dried food, a few cases of MREs, plus the food they had been able to stockpile over the past few weeks, they calculated they had enough for about two months worth of food, and maybe four months if they stretched and rationed it carefully. They would know in a few days, a week at most, if the local and national governments and economic system started recovering, and if they didn't, they thought they could scrounge around and find more food. That would later prove to be a lot more difficult than they imagined.

Both families had stocked up on their prescription medications, as well as having a well-stocked container of emergency medical supplies, including aspirin, vitamins, antiseptics, antibiotics, disinfectants and bandages. They always kept a couple of gallons of bleach on hand to purify their water, and had also stored several long Bic lighters for lighting their BBQ grills and their fireplaces.

But by the following day, it became obvious that the Sea Breezes community was already in some trouble. Several families lost one or both parents who had been killed or injured in various locations around town, especially those that had worked at the refinery. Although the bridge had been damaged, one lane was still open, so most of those adults who were able to return home did so by the next evening. The family across the street had two teenage children at home, but their single dad had worked at the refinery, and the kids feared he might never come home. Sophia went over to check on them, and told them to stay indoors and wait, and that she would look in on them from time to time.

Richard decided to take some action, so he leashed Natasha and walked a few hundred yards over to the home of the HOA president, Fred Carlucci, to sound him out on what the community should do. Fred was a retired teacher in the New York City school district, who had moved south to escape the higher taxes, crime, and the cold weather of New York.

When Fred answered the door Richard said, "Fred, I think we need to have a HOA meeting to discuss what to do about the current situation, especially the homes where there are kids with only one or no parents."

Fred wrinkled his brow and said, "Why? This will all be straightened out by the government in a few days."

"Because, Fred, with the magnitude of the attacks, with D.C. and so many other big cities in a panic over the dirty bombs, things may not be straightened any time soon, and some of the kids need help now. A lot of the families here have parents with jobs in the refinery or on other shift duty. We're checking on Bill Thornton's two kids across the street from us, but if their dad didn't make it, they're going to need some help- they're barely in their teens."

"Well, I suppose it wouldn't hurt. I'll call a meeting of the homeowners." He turned to go inside, and Richard called after him.

"Uh, Fred, how are you going to do that? There's no email or phones working now. We need to get someone on each street to notify all the homes on their street."

"OK, you take care of that and I'll make up an agenda. We'll meet at the church tomorrow morning at 9."

Richard walked down to Josh's house and between them they divided up the streets and went and contacted an adult on each one who was willing to notify all of his neighbors on his street. Each contact was also asked to identify which homes had children with no one to take care of them.

# Chapter 21

The HOA meetings were always held in the basement of the Phelps Island Baptist Church, located near the entrance to Sea Breezes, on Connor Drive. At the meeting the next morning, at least one adult from almost all of the homeowners showed up, and there was standing room only.

Fred opened the meeting with remarks about the current collapse, and that he was sure that everything would be getting back to normal in a few days. All everyone needed to do was stay calm and wait for help.

He then talked about the problem of children in homes with no parents, and a quick count established that there were thankfully only the two Thornton kids, Nichole, 13, and Wayne, 14, and two others; but, there were four other homes where only one parent had made it home and their spouses were missing and unaccounted for. Several of the retired folks promised to do as Sophia had done, and look in on these families from time to time. The other home with parents who had not returned yet had two children under the age of 10, and one of the couples who had no children, and lived next door to them, took them into their home until one of their parents returned, or something permanent could be worked out.

Fred looked pleased at the quick resolution of the problem with the children, and was about to end the meeting when Richard raised his hand to speak.

"Yes, Richard, you want to add something?"

"Yes. I've noticed that many folks who were not able to eat or preserve the contents of their refrigerators and freezers have put the food out in the garbage cans for pickup. But the garbage service didn't come by this morning, and I doubt they will for a long time. Please go though your garbage and pull out the food items and take the bags out the back gate of the community, the one that was supposed to be the entrance to Sea Breezes Phase II, and dump them."

"And please carry them all the way out of the forest to the edge of where the marsh begins. Animals and birds will clean up most of the spoiled food, and it will keep the smell away from our neighborhood, as well as vermin, such as rats.

"If you have any meats left that haven't spoiled, cook them or preserve them. From what I have read, the best way to quickly preserve meat is to cut it in small strips, soak it in brine, and then smoke it on a grill. That should at least keep it edible for a while. Eat your other perishables now if you haven't already, and save your canned goods and preserves for later."

"OK, thanks Richard, anything else before we adjourn?"

Josh stood up and said, "Before the broadcasting stopped we all heard about the dirty bombs and the nation-wide attacks. I doubt the situation is going to improve any time soon. What if the government hasn't recovered in a week or so? What if it takes months for the economy to get back to normal? What are we going to do about security during that time, in case there are problems with looters or robbers? The police who are still on duty have got to be overwhelmed with store looters and crime, and some of that trouble is bound to come our way sooner or later."

There was an anxious murmur among the crowd, and Fred raised his hands for quiet and said, "Don't worry, it won't come to that, and even if it does we can address it at another meeting next week."

Richard shook his head, stood up and said, "Fred, we may not be able to have another meeting next week if things continue the way they are now, and in fact they could get worse at any moment. I would advise everyone with guns to keep them handy, and to stay indoors and locked up tight at night. No one should even think about going shopping- many of you have seen the looting in the shopping centers, so you had better gather your food and supplies and start figuring out how long you can make them stretch. And you can bet that at night there will soon be prowlers out and about looking for opportunities to break in and steal what you have, so everyone should be on their guard."

Fred looked amused and said, "That's just being alarmist. There's no need for guns- we are all civilized. If we all start carrying guns around, we'll just end up shooting each other. The authorities will make sure we are safe."

Josh scoffed and said, "Obviously you weren't down at the Publix, yesterday, Fred. There were looters storming the store and even some gunfire. We need a plan to protect Sea Breezes from people like that, and we need it now." Most of the other homeowners buzzed in agreement, but Fred refused to consider such a thing and declared the meeting over, then got up to leave.

Richard stood up again and said, "Wait a minute. Fred may be the president of the HOA, but these aren't normal times. Fred, if you don't want any part of planning for the safety of the community, there are those of us who do."

Fred said, "Well, go ahead and do whatever you want, but I won't have anything to do with guns or violence." He declared the meeting over again, and walked out, along with a few others. Josh boomed out in his deep voice, "Those of you who are concerned about your own family's safety, as well as the community's, stick around and we can talk about it and set up some kind of plan."

All the rest of the homeowners sat down, and then one man, Jacob Hanson, stood up, and said, "How are we going to do this? Who's going to be in charge?"

Richard stood up and asked if there were any other homeowners who had military or police experience and five men and two women, in addition to Josh and Richard, raised their hands. Richard suggested that each stand up and tell them their experience and training, and he began by giving a quick summary of his Army service. Josh and the rest followed.

Among the veterans, two men were Vietnam vets, but had only served a few years back in the '60s. One of the women had been a police officer for six years before she changed jobs. The rest were veterans of recent wars, but only two had seen actual combat. All volunteered to help in whatever way they could.

Jacob, the man who had asked what they were all going to do stood up again and said, "Look, Richard and Josh both had full careers in the military, so they have the most experience with firearms and security, and I'm sure that they could head up some kind of a security committee for us. Maybe they could organize a plan using the veterans, the gun owners, and anyone else willing to help out- you know, armed patrols of our streets or whatever.

A man named Gary Holmes interrupted and said, "Wait a minute. Just why should we trust them to organize us? Fred says we don't need to do anything anyway."

Richard answered, "Look, you all know that Josh and I disagree with Fred on this. We're worried, and it wouldn't hurt anything to make a plan to organize ourselves to defend our community. As far as qualifications, Josh and I have both had three combat tours over in the Middle East, and every single day we were deployed we had to think about security and defending ourselves, especially at night. I actually had to teach some villagers in Afghanistan to set up defenses of their villages, and Josh was a Drill Sergeant in Marine boot camp. We're just offering our help because of our experience, that's all. We know what needs to be done, but we can't do it all by ourselves.

The rest of the homeowners indicated their agreement, and Jacob called for a vote. Richard and Josh were approved almost unanimously.

Richard stood up again and said, "OK, thanks for the vote of confidence. Between Josh and me, I'm sure we can come up with something workable."

Richard's next question was about how many residents had firearms in their homes to protect them, and a little less than half of the homeowners raised their hands; and as it turned out, a lot of those had only a single shotgun or pistol. This certainly complicated things from a tactical standpoint.

"Anyone who is willing to be part of a security force for Sea Breezes, remain behind and we'll come up with a temporary plan for tonight. We'll need to get a count of who has weapons, and if they have more than one, how many and what type. Also, we need to know if they would go along with loaning them to security duty persons who volunteer but don't have a firearm. Please see Josh after this meeting. I for one will be glad to man a shift on security duty, and to loan out a few of my weapons, and I know Josh will too. If you don't feel comfortable with letting anyone know how many guns you have, no problem, but please consider lending some of them out. You will retain ownership, and once this is over you'll get them back."

"The important thing is that we arm a security force to protect us, and we need to begin tonight. Those that can be on duty tonight stay behind. After we get through here, Josh and I'll go home and figure out a longer-term plan once we know what we have to deal with in the way of resources and people."

"By the way, I don't think we should be congregating outside of Sea Breezes, what with the violence we've already seen, so let's all meet at the picnic area on the lake tomorrow at 9 in the morning. By then we'll have something more concrete to work on. If any of you vets or the police officer, Donna, have any ideas, come see me."

Josh wrote down the names, addresses, and weapons info from all of the homeowners who volunteered, and then asked everyone to leave except those who could perform some security duties starting that evening. Seven men and one woman stayed behind, so counting Richard and Josh, there were 10 of them. One woman approached Richard and introduced herself as Kathryn Brown, and said, "I would like to be part of this, but my husband didn't come home, and our three kids need me around. But I told Josh that we have two pistols, and a shotgun, and I'll be glad to let someone use one of the pistols, but I need to keep a shotgun and a pistol for ourselves. My oldest son, Malcolm, is 16, and he knows how to use both."

Richard said, "That's great, Kathryn, I'll come by your house later and pick up one of your pistols. Make sure your door is locked and don't open it unless you verify it's me or someone you know." Kathryn looked at him and nodded grimly.

# Chapter 22

Richard gathered the volunteers together and laid out his thoughts. "We can't just patrol the streets- that would be suicide at night, as any criminal could just lie in wait and ambush a guy alone on foot. We need to set up positions on roof tops with good observation of the entrance, as well as on some two-story houses near the four corners of the Sea Breezes development, and that also have good lines of sight looking outward. And we need to set up shifts from dawn to dusk, so if you can spend five hours on the first shift or on the second, let me know your preference. We need to have at least one rifle or shotgun on each one of those rooftops." He pulled a map of the community out and after pondering likely avenues of approach other than the obvious single entrance road, selected some houses and made the assignments.

"Make sure you coordinate with the homeowners before you go up on their roof and establish a position. If they object, come and tell me right away so I can make an alternate selection. I doubt that anyone will mind having a personal guard on their roof, but you never know, someone might."

They were able to set up five positions around the community with each position having an assigned five-hour shift covering more or less from dusk to dawn. That would take them through the next meeting of the homeowners the following morning. Richard and Josh went back to the Koenigs' house to come up with a more permanent plan that they would present at the next morning's meeting.

The five positions for that night covered the four corners of the Sea Breezes layout, plus the main entrance, which was, for now, the most likely route for any robbers to take. Richard took the first shift on top of a two-story house near the entrance, with the homeowner's permission, and Josh was his relief. All was quiet that night.

# Chapter 23

The next morning, about 30 men and women showed up at the picnic area, and all brought one or more firearms with them. Richard and Josh had reviewed the initial dispositions of the first night and had made a few adjustments after walking the neighborhood at dawn. They noticed that two of the five rooftop positions didn't respond. One had simply fallen asleep, and the other was missing altogether. The missing man had simply not woken up to relieve the second shift, and the woman on duty who was supposed to be relieved by him just went back to her home after an hour, since she didn't know the address of the man who was to supposed to have relieved her. Richard wasn't surprised at these serious defects, and knew that these situations would be an ongoing problem with an untrained and mostly inexperienced group of civilians; but he also knew that he needed to address the issue at the meeting later on.

At the 9 a.m. meeting, Richard brought up the omissions, without naming names. He just wanted to point out the problem and urge people to be diligent about their duties, set two alarm clocks, and know who their reliefs were, and where they lived. He then went over the refined plan and made up a roster of names and times for each. They had enough volunteers so that each person would serve one five-hour night shift, have a day off, and then pull a day shift. He called another meeting for the next morning, same time and place, to review the plan and get input from the night guards, and hopefully, get more volunteers.

That night they suffered their first casualty. On the southeast corner of the rectangular-shaped development, on the east side of the main entrance where Conner Drive, passed perpendicular to Sea Breezes' entrance road, one of the guards on the second night shift saw two men climb the community fence in his neighbor's yard around midnight. He shouted a warning to stop, and the two intruders froze. The guard then told them to get back over the fence, and as they walked away, he lowered his rifle. But one of the intruders saw this out of the corner of his eye, turned around quickly while pulling his gun, and fired five shots, hitting the guard once, then scrambled back over the fence.

The guard was only lightly wounded, a bullet passing through and through just above his collarbone, but he was too shocked over being hit to return fire, and both of the intruders scrambled over the fence and got away. His wife woke up at the sound of the shots and helped him down the ladder and started treating his wound. Josh was at home and heard the shots. As he was getting dressed, he asked Carmen to go next door to one of his neighbors who was on the guard detail and tell him to grab his gun and meet him in front so they could go check it out.

The two men arrived at the scene a few minutes later, and while Josh checked out the house and talked to the wounded guard, his neighbor reassured the wounded man's wife, and showing clear thinking and without being asked, told Josh he would assume the wounded man's guard position. Josh climbed up the ladder and joined him shortly, and they both scanned outwards looking for any sign of the intruders.

# Chapter 24

At the next morning's meeting, many more homeowners showed up after hearing what had happened the night before. Virtually all of the homeowners were in attendance now, and Richard went over the details for the new defense plan, and the details of the guard positions for the newcomers. He announced that, at least for the next few days, they needed to have daily meetings to discuss schedules, problems, ideas, and events. It was obvious they also needed some form of communication, but cellphones and telephones didn't work. Josh suggested that they canvass the neighborhood for walkie-talkies, even children's versions, and later that afternoon, they came up with three sets, two of them decent models with 5-mile or so ranges.

One of these sets was kept for the guard position at the entrance, and its twin stayed with Josh, since he had assumed the duty of coordinator of the security detail. The other two pair were distributed to the other four positions so each position could talk with one other. Unfortunately, the kid's versions could not be on the same frequency as the commercial sets, but at least they could talk to the nearest guard with its compatible handset.

These things ran on batteries, so they had to set them on the lowest power setting, and in standby modes. The neighborhood then was canvassed for spare batteries, but few were willing to give up the few scarce batteries they had.

It was then that Richard realized they had better have a meeting to discuss a lot more things other than security. So he and Josh contacted their street representatives again and put out the word for another all-homeowners' meeting the next morning at 9, at the picnic area.

The next day there was again standing room only, and Josh called out for everyone to quiet down and listen up. He and Richard had made up a list of subjects to discuss the night before, and Josh took over for the first issue, the current situation on the island.

"We have a lot of things to talk about other than security, since so far we have no indication that any progress has been made toward the national or local situations stabilizing. But first, we need to collect a lot of AA batteries for the walkie-talkies. These are essential for our guards to communicate, and we need all the spares we can get. I know that those of you who have them are reluctant to give them up, since you probably use them for flashlights, but please bring whatever you can spare to tomorrow's meeting, since our security depends on being able to communicate among our guards. Thanks."

Richard stood up and addressed his neighbors on the next subject. "Sophia and I made a trip down to the shopping areas early this morning, but we didn't stop. It looked like most of the stores had been looted, and when we got to the police station we went inside and found it was manned only by the Chief of Police. Five of his officers had radioed in and told the Chief that they were staying at home today to protect their families. Only two police cruisers, with one officer each, were available at the morning roll call. One was sent to block the bridge and screen out intruders and non-residents by checking drivers' licenses; but, he had radioed that he was going to check an approaching convoy of three cars that looked suspicious, and he hadn't been heard from since."

"The other had responded to a lot of gunfire heard over in the Sunset Beach Estates area, and she hadn't responded to his radio calls in over two hours. The Chief feared that both officers, in all likelihood, were either dead or wounded. He was going to remain on duty for a few more hours in case either officer contacted him, but he was planning on heading home to his family if he hadn't heard anything by noon."

"The fire station was vacant except for one man who had stayed behind to monitor the radios, as the two fire trucks and one EMC vehicle had gone out to fight the fires that had engulfed Pelican's Landing. None of the firefighter or EMC crews had responded to radio calls in the past few hours."

"The one small hospital on the island was only partially open, and for severe emergencies only. The ER doctor I spoke to, Dr. Rajan, said that the hospital's staff was dwindling, and that they expected to close down completely by tomorrow if the situation didn't improve. I asked him if we could send a nurse or doctor from the community to gather medical supplies, and after some consideration, he said yes, but whoever came had to show him some form of medical license. We agreed to meet again tomorrow morning at 11."

"Now, I know that there is at least one nurse living here, but I can't remember her name." At that point a woman raised her hand, identified herself as Julia Reed, and said she was an OR nurse. As it turned out, she was the only one in the community with any type of medical license. Richard recognized her now, and remembered that she was single and had no children. He asked her to make up a list of supplies she needed, and asked if she would be willing set up an aid station in her home. She said she would do both, and Richard agreed to pick her up the next morning at 10:45 to drive back to the hospital.

That done, Richard began talking about the next most important but related issue, sanitation. "At some point our water will quit running and our toilets will quit flushing. I know some of you have irrigation wells, and some others have generators. Getting those two resources together will help us out in case we have a prolonged period without rain, but I urge all of you to fill up any containers you have, from bath tubs to buckets to hot tubs, with water while you can.

"If the water goes out before the sewage system stops, you can at least flush your toilets and have enough to drink. Once both go out, we need to establish some way to dispose of our trash, and human waste. The best way to do that is to dig a big hole in your front yard, and I mean a big hole, to dispose of everything. And don't try digging close to trees- you'll spend most of your time cutting through tree roots. Dig in the center of your lawn instead.

You can erect privacy screens around the holes and with a little ingenuity, rig up some kind of toilet seat over the hole. For nighttime, you can use one of two methods- place a large bowl in the toilet, or cut a chair bottom out and nail a toilet seat to it with a bucket underneath. You can empty them the following morning outside into the trash hole."

"I'm serious about this folks- I've seen villages where there was little regard for waste disposal, and disease and unpleasant smells were rife. And I repeat- make those holes big- I'm talking about at least six feet deep and six feet long. I recommend that two neighbors share digging a hole in their front yards. And keep the dirt to sprinkle on top of the, uh, deposits, to minimize flies and odors. And, you'd better not wait until you need them- for all we know, the water and sewage systems could be down now."

"And speaking of generators, I've noticed some homes have been running them off and on, probably to keep their refrigerators and large freezers going. If I were you, I'd stop doing that and save the generators and fuel for emergencies. You need to clean out your freezers and eat the food, or cook it over your BBQ grills, like others have done."

Fred, the former HOA president, was in the audience and he spoke up and said that he was going to run out of food in a week or so, and that the community needed to stockpile all of their food and distribute it equally. Richard and Josh looked at each other and Josh said, "Fred, some of us made investments in buying preserved food, or risked our lives on the day of the attack to go and get more. I agree we need to share food with those in real need, but I won't be giving up all of our food for you or anyone else to hand out to people who made the decision to be unprepared for emergencies, or didn't risk their lives going out on Day 1 to get food when they could."

"What we can do is assist anyone who is short on food by organizing a scavenging trip, with armed escorts, and share the proceeds of whatever we gather equally among those who participate, and among those who for health or childcare reasons are unable to participate. But if you aren't willing to risk going and collecting food, you can't expect others to feed you." Most people understood and agreed, and Fred sat down in a huff.

Josh continued, "Actually, that was the next item on the agenda, and we need to get out there as soon as possible and get what we can before everything is gone. We can hit restaurants, the hospital cafeteria, and other places that may have been overlooked. We can also pry open, knock down, or shoot open any locked storage room doors we come across that others were not able to break into. We're certainly not going to rob anyone, but we will be armed in case anyone tries to attack us or steal things from us. We need to keep the security guys and gals on duty, so we will share whatever we're able to get with them also. Anyone who needs food or other supplies, make a list and show up at the play ground at the lake at 1 p.m. today. Anyone with guns, bring them. We're going to need a strong security detail, just in case anyone gets the idea to jump us."

Richard then took the floor and said, "Speaking of security, we need more volunteers. We ran off several guys who were climbing over the fence along Connor Drive with warning shots early this morning, but we don't have enough people to keep our guard posts manned for an extended period. Those of us on duty are already starting to get tired. We need everyone who is physically able to serve on guard duty, and if you don't have any weapons training, come by my house after tomorrow morning's meeting and I'll take you out to the vacant field behind my house and give you some quick instructions on weapons safety, operation, and firing. If you are going to enjoy the protection of those who are on guard, you need to be part of the effort."

Fortunately, most nodded their heads in agreement, but of course Fred rose up and expressed his disdain for firearms, and declared that he would not be part of any guard force. Richard suggested he think about some other way he could contribute to the community, such as aiding families to dig their trash and latrine holes, or assisting nurse Julia in setting up her home aid station. Fred harrumphed and sat down.

Richard continued, "I'd like to end this meeting, with some good news. Bill Thornton made it home last night, so he's back with his kids. One other missing man, Kathryn Brown's husband, also came in early this morning. I talked to both of them and they said that they had to lay low and work their way back to and across the bridge carefully, as the inner city of Port Monroe was erupting in rioting and looting, and there were exchanges of gunfire heard all over town."

"Police cars were burned and they saw several dead policemen, along with a lot of dead civilians. No one is checking people coming back over the bridge any more, and it's only a matter of time before more trouble comes looking for us. We all need to have a sense of urgency about getting things done as quickly as possible."

By the time the meeting was over, Richard was dog tired, and he went home and lay down on the couch for a few minutes. Sophia sat down and put his head in her lap, looked at him and said, "Rick, you and Josh can't do this all by yourselves. If you're worn out you won't be good for anything, and you might even fall asleep on guard duty. I'm going to take your guard shift tonight. I talked to Carmen and she's going to do the same for Josh. You both have got to get some sleep."

Richard started to protest, but he knew she was right. "I know, Hon, but we've got to get things set up right. We are nowhere near having all the security problems ironed out, and that's going to take us a few more days. In a few minutes I've got to take Julia Reed over to the hospital to get whatever medical supplies we can talk the ER doc out of. That's a big priority."

"When I get home I've got go out on a food-scavenging mission with the homeowners. Josh is planning a route to take, and he's also figuring out security for the convoy. We can't just go wandering over the whole island, because we need to save our gas. I'll grab something to eat when I get back from the hospital, but then I've got to meet everyone at the lake. And tomorrow I've got to start digging our trash hole. Sooner or later we're going to need it."

## Chapter 25

Julia Reed was a divorcee with no children. She was a tall, good-looking young woman, with short blonde hair and beautiful green eyes. She was a few pounds overweight, but she had jokingly told Richard on their drive out to the hospital that she had already started on a diet, as of Day 1. She had a very pleasant personality, and an air of confidence about her that Richard liked.

Julia had worked in a hospital in Port Monroe but was off shift when the nation-wide attacks began, and she knew better than to try to get back across the bridge for her evening shift that day. She was a very caring nurse at heart, and wanted to help out in the best way she could. Living alone made it easy for her to volunteer her home as an aid station, and she believed, as did Richard, that she would have more and more to do as time went on.

When they arrived at the little Phelps Island hospital, Richard drew his pistol and let it hang by his side as they entered the ER. No one was there but a nurse who had volunteered to stay until noon, waiting for Richard to come by. Richard introduced himself and started to tell her about his meeting Dr. Rajan the day before.

She interrupted and said, "He remembered you and your wife stopping by, and before he left he put together two boxes of supplies for you. But you're welcome to look around and take anything else you think you can use.

"Poor guy, Dr. Rajan has been working around the clock. Did you know that he was a Muslim from India? He's ashamed and disgusted by what is being done in the name of his religion, and it seems like he feels that he has to make up for as much as he can all by himself.

"He was exhausted this morning and finally went home, and I'm the last of the hospital staff still here. I hope he got home O.K. Anyway, you'll have to hurry because I've got to get back home to my kids as soon as possible."

Julia nodded her head in understanding and said, "Give us 15 minutes, and we'll be out of here. Do you need a ride home?"

"No thanks. I have my car and I live just a few blocks away in the Camellia apartments."

While Richard loaded the boxes, she went into the ER and started gathering up some instruments and other equipment. Richard told her to hurry it up, as he didn't want to stick around any longer than necessary with just him as security. Julia looked around in a couple of the ground floor supply rooms and in cabinets, but didn't find much left. Obviously the staff had used up a lot of supplies and equipment, or taken home everything that they wanted. She came out with one more box overflowing with stuff. Richard was grateful that doc Rajan was a man of his word.

When they pulled into Julia's driveway, Julia got out and opened the front door while Richard hauled in the first box. He saw that Julia had already been thinking and working on her aid station concept. She had a few dining room chairs in the living room, and her dining room table was covered with a plastic pad and sheets to use as an "operating" table. Julia started sorting through the boxes and putting things in their place, so he figured he might as well head back home, pick up Sophia, and get ready for the scavenging mission.

# Chapter 26

Richard was pleased that when they arrived at the lake, Josh already had the people who arrived early lined up, and ready to go. Once everyone was there Josh called them all together and told them the general route they would follow, gave them the details of the plan, and laid out the security rules.

"Folks, let's understand that when we get back, Richard and I will divide up everything we get, setting aside nine piles of stuff for families that couldn't be here today for various reasons. Everyone else who comes with us gets an equal per person or family share. I think I told them all, but if any of you are single parents don't come. We'll save a share for you. Also if there are any couples here that have kids who are all under 18, only one of you can come, just in case something happens. There will be only two people in each car or truck so we can load in as much stuff as possible.

"Our first stop will be in the shopping center with the Wal-Mart and Publix, and we'll start on the end at the Wal-Mart. If any of you have any medicines you need, go to the pharmacy and look for them. Also, pick up things like disinfectants, first aid supplies, and bandages that are left. Julia will be with us to pick up anything specific that she needs.

"There is no way for me to know exactly what each family is short of, so take those items you need first and put them in your lawn and garbage bags and when they are filled, head back to the cars, grab another bag, and go back into the store. Keep your personal bag with you so I can make sure you get the things that you need when I divide up the items we get. And make sure you save those bags and any boxes you brought along, or that we find in the stores. We will be reusing them a lot from now on.

"When we get to each store, Richard and I will go in first with our shotguns and make sure the area is clear. I'll then guard the rear door and Richard will guard the front. The drivers of the first and last cars will stay with the vehicles and keep a lookout. Make sure everyone who knows how to use a gun has one. I've brought some extras of mine if you don't have one."

When they departed, they had 14 vehicles and 28 people. Richard was surprised to see Fred Carlucci there, but he refused to carry a gun. Richard shrugged his shoulders rather than get into an argument, and they took off, with Josh's car leading the way.

They arrived at the Wal-Mart and noticed all the windows were broken and the doors open. As Richard and Josh entered, they saw a man and a woman run out the back door carrying some full laundry bags. Josh yelled to them to come back, that they wouldn't be hurt, but they were out the door and gone. As it turned out, there was very little left on the shelves. Although the pharmacy had been looted for narcotic drugs, most people in need of real medicine, such as blood pressure and diabetes medications, found what they needed. Apparently they were the first group to enter in a systematic and protected manner, and most of their medical and pharmaceutical needs were met.

This was not a super Wal-Mart with a grocery store, and there was no food left among the items still on the shelves and by the cash registers. Josh was at the rear door and noticed a locked storeroom at the back of the store near the loading ramp. It was locked with a heavy-duty internal lock, and he called for Richard to come and take a look. They had no idea what might have been inside, but they decided to try and open the door. Josh loaded his twelve-gage shotgun with magnum slug rounds and after firing three rounds into the locking system, Richard was able to pry open the door with a crowbar.

Inside they found stacked boxes of canned, ready-to-serve food and soups, snacks, and things like batteries and paper products. This was a true windfall, and the gatherers took everything and loaded it up in the cars and trucks.

Then they drove over to Publix, where they found pretty much the same thing. The pharmacy did yield a few of the more of the essential medications needed, including several types of antibiotics that Julia discovered. But there was no food, paper products, or anything they really needed left anywhere. Obviously, those who had taken a chance and ventured out after Day 1 had cleaned the store out. The back of the store was filled with mostly rotting fruits, vegetables, and dairy products. The Publix was an obvious place to scavenge so it turned out to be pretty much a disappointing waste of time.

Next they went on to the Home Depot at the far end. Here there was plenty of plywood, nails, glue, lumber, and some BBQ essentials, as well as a couple of generators. There was so much stuff they could use that half of the larger vehicles that were already filled with scavenged items were sent back to Sea Breezes to unload and return to pick up the rest of the hardware and supplies they thought might prove useful. To Richard's surprise, even Fred seemed to work fairly well at getting things loaded onto the trucks and SUVs.

But after the larger vehicles left, a heavy duty pickup roared in to the parking lot with guns blazing from three men in the pickup bed and one in the cab. This was followed by another pickup with two men in the back firing. Obviously they had been watching the Sea Breezes scavengers awhile, and seeing that they had been able to load up a lot of food and other items, the attackers had waited until the larger, more heavily guarded vehicles left before they launched their surprise assault, hoping to catch them by surprise.

Two of the homeowners guarding the vehicles were killed immediately, as they were standing out in the open. Josh and Richard were used to this sort of attack and reacted quickly laying down a heavy base of fire with their semi-auto shotguns, and a few other homeowners, after recovering from their shock and initial paralysis, returned fire also. The attackers hadn't expected this quick of a reaction, and decided to flee the kill zone. The first truck was stopped under the hail of fire, and all the occupants were riddled with bullets. The second pickup got away, but Josh noted that at least the two men in the bed of the pickup were hit, if not killed.

As for the Sea Breeze contingent, one of the other drivers was killed and three of the gatherers were wounded, one badly. This had been a costly expedition for the homeowners; a total of three killed, all men, and three wounded, including one woman.

It was a grim and fast trip home to the picnic area, and there were women waiting who found out their husbands were killed or wounded. It was a sorrowful sight and a very bad time.

All of the casualties had been loaded into the last vehicles, with room made for the three wounded in the back of three cars. These cars sped off to Julia's home aid station first, and six men carried the three wounded into her home. One of the men had been a combat veteran in Iraq, and stayed to help her with caring for the wounded. Julia lived next door to Bill Thornton's house and she sent one of the men over to get him and his teenage children to come and help. Bill and his daughter, Nichole, and son, Wayne, arrived in minutes and Julia started barking orders to them. They were in for a long night.

Back at the picnic area, shock and disbelief set in among the scavenging party. One man, overloaded with adrenaline, went out to the road and vomited. Richard and Josh went around and checked on everyone else to see if they were OK. They were all very shaken up, but still functioning.

As the sun was setting, Josh and Richard knew they needed to put everyone to work doing something useful, as the best way to get them over the psychological trauma they had endured, so they enlisted their help to begin sorting out the provisions into more or less even piles, including those for the single parent homes, and the roof top guards, as well as extra portions for the families who had lost someone. Another pile of the material they had gotten at Home Depot, mostly hardware and wood, as well as one generator, was locked up in the picnic area's storeroom for later distribution or community use. After the sorting was accomplished, Josh reminded everyone of the guard schedule, and he had to make some last minute substitutions for the two casualties who had been scheduled for later guard duty.

As night fell, everyone headed for home to unload their goods, and to hand out the shares to the single parents, guards' families, and disabled that lived nearby. Then they went home and told their loved ones and neighbors what happened, and got some much needed rest.

After offloading their shares of the supplies, and filling in their families on what had transpired, both Josh and Richard headed to bed and fell into a deep sleep. Fortunately, that night there were no security incidents.

# Chapter 27

Richard woke at daybreak, refreshed but troubled. He took a cold shower, went to the bathroom and flushed the toilet. As he got out of the shower, he smelled eggs and bacon cooking on the BBQ grill, and smiled. Sophia had served the second shift of guard duty, came home, and cooked up the last of the bacon and eggs for their breakfast. She had a pot of coffee going also, and they sat down at the kitchen table for a welcomed and almost normal breakfast. They had finished washing the dishes, and just as they began rinsing them, the water quit running. The pipes knocked and expelled air, and the dribble of water slowed to an increasingly slower drip.

Sophia looked at Richard and said, "Oh no!" Richard hugged her as tears came to their eyes. They both knew that this meant a big change for the worse for the community.

A 9 a.m. meeting at the picnic area had now become a daily ritual. Almost the entire community was there to hear the details of what had happened on the scavenger hunt the day before. Richard told everyone who hadn't already heard what had occurred. Bill Thornton was there and informed everyone that one of the wounded had died, and that Julia had said they needed to bury all of the dead this morning. Richard suggested the empty field behind his house, and 12 volunteers were selected for burial detail. He told them to make sure they buried everyone at least 5-6 feet deep, and as far away as they could before the field turned into woods.

At the meeting, one of the men of the five couples who had not participated in the scavenging trip demanded they be given part of the food the group had gathered- he said he wanted his "fair share." Richard stared him down and said coldly, "I told you that only people who risked making the trip would get to share in the spoils. You all decided not to participate, so you get nothing. You will not take from others who risked their lives, some of whom died or were wounded, to bring back food to their families. If you want anything you will have to come out on our next trip this afternoon. Otherwise, sit down and shut up."

This enraged the man and he got in Richard's face yelling and screaming. When Josh stepped in and pulled him away, he took a swing and glanced a punch off of Josh's cheekbone. Josh struck back with a right cross to the jaw that decked the man, as his wife screamed and ran to her husband's side, yelling obscenities at Josh and Richard.

Richard looked at the wife and the other four couples and said, "If you want food, be here at one o'clock this afternoon. We will go to the Target shopping center. Anyone else who went out yesterday and still needs more can come also, but that will be the last trip we take for a while. As you all know by now, the water is off. You may still be able to flush toilets with any water you've saved, but you had best get busy digging your garbage and latrine holes now if you haven't already. And by the way, the lake water is absolutely off limits, as our ducks, geese, and other waterfowl around it have to be sustained. We will be killing them and eating them soon as our food runs out, so don't screw up their habitat or pollute the water by washing or bathing. Let's go home and get to work digging, and those who want to go scavenging to the Target shopping center be here with your cars and your guns at one o'clock." Everyone departed and many went out with the families of the deceased to help dig the graves, and mourn for their lost friends and neighbors.

# Chapter 28

Only 11 cars showed up for the afternoon scavenger hunt, including the men of the families who did not go out on the first hunt. It's not that there weren't a lot of families that needed food; it was that too many were afraid of getting killed after seeing the results of the last expedition. Richard knew that was a mistake and shortsighted, but there was nothing he could do about it.

He and Josh gave the same instructions as the day before, with two modifications: all the vehicles would stay together at all times. No car or person would stray from the group for any reason, and there would be one shooter remaining behind with each car for security. The remaining 11 men and women would go in together and clear the store first, with Josh and Richard again standing guard at the back and front entrances while the gatherers looked for food and other essentials.

They first went back to the Home Depot and gathered up the items they had intended to bring back yesterday. Then they went on to the Target strip mall. Since this shopping center did not have any grocery store attached, it hadn't been raided as much, and they actually found cases of food, mostly snacks, canned soup and quick lunches, high up on the back shelves of the Target's storage area. They had to find some ladders to get them down, but the food was another windfall. They also were fortunate to find a couple of sets of walkie-talkies, and some batteries, which would greatly enhance their ability to communicate with the guards, especially at night.

There was a Mexican restaurant in the center of the strip mall where they found several gallon-sized containers of cooking oil, various spices, salt, canned tomato sauce, beef and chicken stock, as well as cartons of corn flour, rice, and beans. All of these items were loaded up also.

At the opposite end there was a small ACE hardware store where they were able to pick up some shovels and picks, batteries, and other tools and hardware. Richard passed by an aisle that had vegetable seeds, then thought for a second and returned and got all that were on the shelves, because you never knew. It may be February, but if the situation continued to worsen, they might need to plant gardens.

On the way back home they took a different route and passed Leroy Ivory's 7/11. It had been burned to the ground. Since they were in the area, they swung by Leroy's home to check on him. The old Marine vet's house showed some bullet holes in the windows and the bricks of his home, and there was blood all over the front yard. Josh called out to Leroy from the curb, and waited until Leroy opened the door, to ask how he was doing.

"Not so good, Josh. Some looters came by the night before last and I had to run them off with my 12 gauge. They shot through the windows and hit my wife, Althea, in the wrist, and she's not doing well. I think it's starting to get infected."

Josh looked at Richard and raised his eyebrows in an unspoken question. Richard understood and nodded, so Josh said, "Leroy, I think there is an empty home in Sea Breezes that you can move into- one of the bachelors in the neighborhood was killed yesterday, and I don't believe he has anyone living with him. We'll check it out and if it's empty you can move in; if not, you can stay in our guest bedroom until there's a vacancy. We also have an aid station of sorts, and Althea can get her hand treated by our nurse."

Leroy looked over at his wife and Althea nodded her head yes. Leroy let out a big sigh and said "O.K., Josh, we'll come with you. And thanks."

"Good. Gather up everything you want to take with you and load it in your truck and car. I doubt you'll be coming back here any time soon, so get everything useful, especially all your food, medical supplies, and your two weapons and the ammo. Bring your stuff out and set it on the porch. We'll help you load up your car and truck, but we can only stay another 10 minutes or so before we have to get out of here. I'll get one of our guys to drive your truck, and you can drive your car and Althea can ride with you."

Twelve minutes later, 13 vehicles set out for Sea Breezes and as they were leaving, they heard gunfire back on the far side of Leroy's neighborhood. Everyone sped up and got back to Sea Breezes and the picnic area quickly.

It was raining when they got back, so Josh and Richard directed everyone to unload the vehicles, except for the Ivorys' car and truck, and pile the goods under the picnic area's roof. Josh led the Ivorys to the vacant house, and they waited in their car while Josh went up to the door and knocked. There was no answer, so he went next door and asked the neighbor if the man there had lived alone. His neighbor said yes, although he had a girlfriend that stayed over often, but apparently they had broken up several months ago, since she hadn't been around for a while.

Josh returned to Leroy and said, "Leroy, we'll have to break a window to get in, but it looks almost certain that the house is unoccupied. You unload your truck and the car, and move your stuff inside, and after we get in I'll take Althea in my car to our aid station."

Leroy nodded and as Althea switched over to Josh's car, the two men broke a side window and crawled in. The house was surprisingly tidy, and there was a decent supply of food. There was no sign of anyone having lived in any of the other two rooms, and the master bedroom's bed had only one side in disarray, indicating the deceased man who had lived there was alone. Josh said goodbye, and headed out to the car and on to the aid station, leaving Leroy to unload his food and gear from his vehicles.

Meanwhile, Richard and several others from the expedition set out some items for the single parent and guard families again, and divided up the rest in equal piles. He announced that he and Josh would forego their shares so that the remainder could have more. This pleased everyone, especially the husbands who had not gone out on the first run, although one complained that there were some things in his pile that he didn't want.

Richard thought, "Tough shit," but instead he said, "Don't worry. Tomorrow morning at the 9 o'clock meeting, I'll announce a flea market and swap meet for tomorrow afternoon. We'll have it right after lunch all around the lake area, so people can trade items they don't want or need among themselves. I'll be bringing several cans of beets and turnip greens I want to get rid of."

That actually got a laugh from the group, and relieved some of the tension. Since Josh was gone, Richard reminded everyone of the evening's guard duty assignments. After all of the food had been separated, with no other meetings or outings scheduled for the day, Richard went home, and along with the rest of the homeowners, spent the rest of the day digging their trash holes, inventorying and organizing their supplies, and resting.

# Chapter 29

After leaving Leroy to unload his car and truck, Josh pulled into the driveway and helped Althea out of the car. Julia had seen them pull up, and opened the front door for them. She took one look at Althea's bandaged wrist, told her to have a seat at the kitchen dinette table, and went about cleaning her wound with the help of young Nichole Thornton, who had turned out to be a natural nurse, eager to learn. Josh asked Julia about the other patients, as in addition to the wounded, two children had been brought in with food poisoning, probably from eating spoiled food. Julia said that Bill and his kids were taking turns looking in on them, changing bandages, and otherwise helping out.

Bill was there now and he came over and told Josh that it looked as if the sick and wounded remaining in the house might all recover, thanks to Julia's expert treatment, the medical supplies they had gotten from the hospital, and the antibiotics they had recovered from the pharmacy. Bill told Josh he thought that he and his kids might just become permanent assistants to Julia, as it looked as if they would be having more patients as time went on.

Several other residents had already been by the aid station with minor ailments, and one parent had brought in a child with a fractured forearm, which Julia was able to splint and wrap. Josh agreed with Bill's assessment, and said he hoped the arrangement worked out for them all.

Bill added one more thing. "Josh, we need to get a generator and some extension cords for lights. We have to check regularly on our patients, including during the night, and we are running low on flashlight batteries. Besides, sometimes we need more light than we can get from a small flashlight, especially if in the future we have casualties at night that need to be treated right away."

"I'll get on it and have a generator up here before dark. Can you get some long extension cords?"

"Yes, I have some at home, and we won't need more than a couple of plug outlets bars, for several lights, so we won't be putting much of a load on the generator. We'll also be able to charge up rechargeable batteries while it's running. If you could round us up all the rechargeable batteries with their chargers from the neighbors, we can use the generator very efficiently."

"That's good, Bill, but use it sparingly. I'll get the generator we have in the picnic area's storage room and be back here with it and some gas and oil in an hour or so."

# Chapter 30

In the early morning hours, shortly after midnight, two carloads of gang members drove up to the front of the Sea Breezes' entrance. They got out of their cars, reached in for their rifles and shotguns, and started heading for the community's entrance. The guard on the roof near the entrance saw what was happening, and after a brief hesitation, started firing his AR-15 rifle as fast as he could pull the trigger. He switched magazines after the first 30 rounds were fired, and started firing again.

The gangbangers were taken by surprise, not expecting trouble before even entering the development, and at first they had difficulty telling where the fire was coming from. In the confusion, five of them had been hit by the guard's fire and were on the ground, wounded or dead. Two others tried to load one of the wounded back in the car while the others finally located the rooftop guard position and wildly returned fire against the guard.

But the guard position had been fortified with pillowcases filled with rocks and dirt, which gave the guard some protection from the gang's inaccurate fire. He was able to pick off one of the men carrying the wounded gang member, and the other gangbanger dropped the wounded man and dove into the lead car. The car sped off, leaving behind six men dead or wounded, and one car.

The guard took out his walkie-talkie, called Josh and told him briefly what had happened. Josh, lived close to the entrance, and had been awakened by all the firing and was already up and dressing when he called. Richard had also been woken up by the firing, and came running as fast as his gimpy leg would let him, carrying his rifle and pistol, and one of the new walkie-talkies. He radioed Josh to let him know he was coming. Josh was already on the scene with his shotgun trained on the fallen gangbangers when Richard arrived. Josh yelled at the six men on the ground and told them to lie still or they would be shot.

Josh yelled up to the guard for him and Richard to cover him, and to shoot anyone who moved. He handed Richard his shotgun and drew his .45 cal. Kimber semi-auto pistol and approached slowly, telling everyone on the ground to freeze or that he and the others would shoot at any movement. He cautiously and carefully checked each one and found that four of the men were definitely dead. One of the two left alive was barely conscious, and probably dying from wounds in the leg and chest. The remaining man, the one who had been shot last by the guard as he tried to help his buddy into the car, had been hit in the side. He would probably live only a day or two unless he got some decent medical care.

Josh was not inclined initially to offer him any medical assistance, but after clearing all guns from the two living men, and other guns around the area, Josh holstered his pistol and tore his T-shirt off and into strips, and wrapped the wounded man's side to staunch the bleeding. Josh looked over at Richard and raised his eyebrows. The question was understood, and Richard nodded his head, yes- let him live.

Richard approached the young man Josh was working on, with his Bersa 9 mm semi-auto pointed at the thug's head and asked him, "What's your name, and what name does your gang go by?"

"The young man grimaced in pain and replied, "My name's Marcus. We from the Zulu Warriors."

"We heard a lot of firing over towards Sunset Beach Estates yesterday. Were you the people who were shooting over there?"

"Yeah, that was the Zulus. But I didn't go with them since I had to look after my momma and my sisters back in Port Monroe. The Zulus figured that was where the money was, and that they'd be easy pickin's. And they was right. From what I heard, they pretty much cleaned them out. We're set up there now and are using it as our home base."

"Why did the whole gang move out to Sunset Beach?"

"We had to get out of Port Monroe. That town turned into a stinkin' shithole, and there was so much shootin' and lootin', it was costin' us too many men to defend our turf. The Zulus went and took a real nice place to set up and I moved my family out there this morning. Look, I didn't hurt none of you guys, so please don't shoot me."

"We'll see. Before I decide, I have another question you had better answer truthfully if you want to live. How many of you are there?"

"I dunno 'zactly- maybe about 70 or so men, women, and children in all, and about 30 or so Warriors. Less now."

"Listen to me, Marcus. I'll make you a deal. We won't kill you and we'll let you go now. But take this message to your brothers: we let you live because we don't want any trouble, and we have no intention of reprisals against your gang as long as they leave us alone. Stay away from our community, because we are well armed and well guarded, 24/7. We know you're out there now and next time we will be even better prepared."

"OK, I can do that."

"We're going to load up your dead in the trunk and back seat, and your other wounded buddy in the front seat, and let you drive back to Sunset beach. You'd better hurry because the guy that'll be in the front seat is dying, and you'll bleed out soon if you don't get some help."

They loaded everyone in the car, and although it had taken some rounds that had shot out one headlight and put holes through the windows and doors, Marcus was able to get the car started and in gear. He then turned around, and sped off. Richard wondered if he'd make it back to Sunset Beach before he bled to death.

Richard and Josh walked back to the house and took the ladder up to the roof to talk to the guard. The guard turned out to be the guy who had thrown the punch at Josh the morning before. His name was Martin Goldman and he was sitting down near the bags of rocks and dirt, shaking like a leaf. Josh went over and sat down next to him.

"Martin, good job tonight. You did the right thing by opening up on them as soon as you saw them pull out their guns. You probably saved a lot of lives tonight. You OK?"

"I got a few cuts on my chest and arms from splintered rocks in the pillowcases that were hit by their return fire, but nothing serious."

"Look, your shift is almost over, so go on down to the aid station and get your cuts treated. I'll cover your duty until dawn. Please be at the 9 o'clock meeting later this morning so you can tell everyone what happened here. We obviously need to discuss this attack and how to plan for the next one. We may not be as lucky the next time as we were this morning."

"Thanks, Josh, and... well... thanks." Martin got up, walked to the edge of the house, climbed down the ladder, and headed over to Julia's house.

Richard and Josh sat there and rearranged the three bags that had probably saved Martin's life. Richard looked over and said, "Josh, we got lucky tonight. If Martin hadn't been alert, and if he hadn't shot the hell out of those guys right from the start, we could have really had a problem. We need to come up with some type of quick reaction force, and train them to respond to incidents like this one. The next gang that tries to attack us might be bigger, and hit us from a less obvious location, and if they are from the Zulu Warriors, they will now know what to expect. I'm almost sorry we didn't just shoot those two guys left alive now, but I don't think we've sunk to that level yet."

Josh nodded and said, "Yeah. But setting up a reaction force in a community of civilians is going to be a lot easier said than done. Let's do some thinking about it. You go ahead on back to Sophia, and please stop off and let Carmen know I'm OK."

Richard said he would, then patted his friend on the back and took off.

# Chapter 31

Almost every household in the neighborhood was at the 9 o'clock meeting, all abuzz about what happened during the night, or rather the early morning. Rumors were flying and people were worried.

Josh stood up and said, "Attention everyone. Let's get the first item of business out of the way and explain what went on last night. I'm going to turn this over to Martin who will tell you exactly what unfolded while he was on guard duty."

Martin stood up and explained the sequence of events while the homeowners sat there with their mouths open. Josh then related what happened when he and Richard arrived on the scene, including the fact that Sunset Beach Estates had apparently been pretty much wiped out and occupied by the Zulu Warrior gang. The crowd gasped at this. Some of them had friends who had lived in Sunset Beach.

Richard was next and said, "Listen, we were very lucky. If it hadn't been for Martin's vigilance, quick reaction, and good shooting, several houses might have been hit and a lot of people killed.

"It's obvious now that due to the expanding threats, we've got to set up some kind of a quick reaction force for situations like this. I don't mean a group of armed men staying awake at night, but we do need a rotating list of five armed homeowners that are ready to go out every night whenever they hear gunfire. I thought this over last night and the five need to be all on the same street or general area, with a designated rendezvous point nearby, and then move out tactically to the area being attacked. This will take a little training, so Josh and I will start making up rosters of men and women who aren't single parents, including any children 18 or over living at home, and we'll begin some basic training in the field behind my house, taking two groups at a time. I figure we have enough people for four groups of quick reaction forces, and we can spread them out over the community to cover attacks from any side.

"No one is exempt from this duty," and he looked over and stared at Fred Carlucci, who just looked away. Richard decided he had better get this out of the way now, and said, "Fred, you or anyone else who has resisted being a part of the guard force will no longer be given a free ride. You'll be part of a quick reaction force, and I'll spend some time with you and anyone else who has never fired a rifle tomorrow, before the rest of your group arrives for tactical drill. Anyone who is able-bodied and refuses to serve will be shunned and cut off from support by the community. Is that clear?"

Fred hung his head and mumbled something under his breath.

Richard got in his face and said, "What did you say?"

Fred, recoiled and answered, "Nothing.... I'll be there."

Richard nodded and said, "Good. We have to do the training in two stages so that each one of the two parents in a family attends a training session. Josh and I will need some time to complete the rosters, and to set up a training area in the field behind my house. We'll begin tomorrow morning after the 9 a.m. meeting with the first group and then with the second group at one o'clock. Everyone bring all your rifles and pistols to the meeting in the morning and be ready to go in case you are in the morning training group."

"Now, those single parents who aren't going to be pulling any security duty will need to help out those who are. Walking around the area I've noticed that everyone has holes for disposing of waste and trash, but some of them are pretty puny. During the daylight, I expect those men and women who are not serving on some type of security duty, and all older children, to help the guard force expand their holes while they are on guard or sleeping. You can also help out at the aid station or pick up trash around the area. I'll leave it up to the families to get this done, but bear in mind that everyone has to cooperate, and contribute to all the work that needs to be done in order for us to survive, both as a community, and individually."

"We have one more thing to discuss this morning. I know that some of you are running short of specific items of food, paper products, or other supplies. So, we're going to have a sort of flea market and swap meet this afternoon at one o'clock around the lake. Go home and make up your 'shopping list' of needs and wants, then pack up everything you can or want to trade, and come back here after lunch. Besides food, think about things such as batteries, tools, clothing, gas, containers, pots, BBQ grills, firewood, paper products, plastic ware, shoes and boots, raingear, coats, and such that you would be willing to trade for something you need."

If you have extra guns or ammunition, you can bet you'll be able to trade for those and get a good exchange. And, speaking of batteries, everyone with rechargeable batteries of any size, including car batteries, take them and their chargers to Julia and Bill at the aid station for recharging when they run their generator. Mark them with your names and they'll return them to you after they've been charged. If you can spare a few, leave them for Julia and Bill, as they need them for flashlights to check on their patients at night."

"For the swap meet or flea market, or whatever you want to call it, each family bring a blanket and lay out your wares. At least two family members should come, one to bargain and one to shop. Have a list of what you want to shop for, and you can walk around to everyone else's blanket and if you see something you need and can trade for."

"Also, consider trading for work as well as goods, especially if you have a craft or talent, like sewing, or repairing tools, sharpening knives, or carpentry, or just providing a strong back to move or carry things."

"While you're at it, think about reinforcing your home's windows and doors with wood, furniture or bags of sand, dirt, or rocks. We can get a lot of material from those partially built homes in Phase II, if you haven't already thought of that. Those are some more items you might want to use for trade."

Julia raised her hand, and when Richard nodded, she stood up and said, "I just wanted to give everyone a report on the aid station status and our patients. First, and most important, all of the wounded, including newcomer Althea Ivory, are doing well and will recover."

Cheers erupted, and shouts of "Way to go, Julia," and "Thank God" rang out from the crowd to hear the good news about their friends and neighbors.

Julia smiled and continued, "Right now, Bill Thornton and his kids are helping me every day, but we need medical supplies. I know everyone wants to keep some first aid items and medications on hand for themselves, but please scour your homes for things like extra disinfectants, bandages, antibiotic ointments, and medications you have extra or no longer need. I'll be at the covered picnic table area this afternoon, so please stop by there and drop off whatever we can use at the aid station. Remember, many of you have already used our aid station, and many more undoubtedly will in the future, so it's to your advantage for us to have on hand what we need to treat you."

"And one last thing. Some of you know that Bill and I have decided to move in together. I love him and his kids, and they love me. I know this seems all very sudden and rushed, but we have known each other for a long time and there has always been an attraction between us; and, let's face it, these are not normal times."

The crowd hooted and applauded and Julia's face turned red, but Bill stood up and gave her a hug and a quick kiss, to more hoots and whistles from their neighbors. They both sat down together with big grins on their faces.

Richard smiled and said, "Congratulations, Julia and Bill. We all wish you as much happiness as possible in these troubled times." He waited until the crowd quieted down and continued, "Now, there will be other things that the community will need to do together. We need to block off the entrance with a barricade of cars and obstacles. We can always move one of the cars if we have the chance to go out on another scavenging trip, but you can imagine there is not much left out there to be had, so we also need to plan on making a garden, or gardens, to contribute to our future food needs."

"I was able to pick up some vegetable seeds from ACE hardware, and I know it's a bit too early to do any planting, but you can at least start some seedlings indoors. Some of you have small gardens in your back yard, so anyone with expertise, and spare seeds, please come and see Sophia this afternoon. She'll be there next to Julia in the covered picnic area and she'll listen to ideas on where and how to plant a community garden, or a plan for several smaller gardens to help feed the community. Bring her your ideas and she can discuss them with you."

"Also, we have some tools, wood and other materials locked up in the picnic area storage shed. We need to think about reinforcing our rooftop guard positions, and building alternate ones on other rooftops that we can use since our current positions are probably being watched. We will start rotating those positions as soon as we set them up. Anyone with extra pillowcases or other cloth bags or plastic bags, please bring them to me tomorrow at the picnic shed. We can fill them with dirt, sand, rocks, wood, or anything that will stop a bullet, and use them to give our guards more protection."

With that, Richard reminded everyone to set up around the lake after lunch, and adjourned the meeting until the next morning. He then went home and sat in the living room lounge chair and fell asleep almost immediately.

# Chapter 32

The name everyone finally settled on as the day progressed was the "Sea Breezes Bazaar," and it would become a frequent event over time; however, everyone knew that none of the following bazaars would be as big as the first one, as everyone's food stores and supplies would begin to dwindle.

Everything began well. Families set up in an orderly fashion and in an almost festive mood. A lot of goods and services were exchanged, and almost as important, the community came together again with a renewed sense of relative normality. Kids of all ages, and Natasha and other dogs, played on the playground, as the adults swapped and bargained good-naturedly, for no one was as of yet in dire straits.

The festive mood of the residents was helped by one of the new widows who had brought several bottles of liquor that she was trading by the shot for small amounts of food or other items she needed. She neither smoked nor drank, and she was also trading off her husband's cigarettes, often a few cigarettes at a time. After about an hour into the start of the bazaar, one man actually gave her a box of canned food in exchange for the two and a half cartons of cigarettes she had left. Richard was nearby and was occasionally glancing over and saw her last transaction. He thought to himself that old addictions died hard, but pretty soon all smokers would be quitting cold turkey.

Sophia and Carmen had been making a list of items they could trade, and another one of things they wanted or needed. Carmen said to Sophia, "You know, with two kids we are already out of toilet paper. It's hard to make them get used to conserving anything, especially TP. I doubt that anyone will be trading for toilet paper tomorrow, but if you see some, let me know."

"Well, I have hoarded one of those mega packs of Charmin as part of our "what if" supplies, so I can let you have a few rolls. We have already started gathering up our phone books and junk mail catalogues, but pretty soon we will have to resort to leaves or something. Funny how you never plan enough for some of the things you take for granted in the modern world."

Carmen smiled and thanked her. They gathered up their supplies and took them over to the lake and set up their own blankets. Richard wasn't kidding about the beets and the turnip greens, and brought a can of each to trade. Sophia made sure she kept one of each for herself though. She liked them even if Richard didn't.

The Koenigs and the Cantrells were probably among the best prepared as far as food, weapons and ammo went, but since they both had fireplaces, they were able to trade some canned food for a nice stockpile of firewood. They also traded some ammunition, but only to individual homeowners who were running low.

Both Richard and Josh had contributed many of their weapons and a lot of their ammunition to be used by the guard force, a sacrifice they decided was in the best interest of them all. But they also made sure they remained personally well armed. Each family kept one semi-auto shotgun, one semi-auto rifle with several 30 round magazines, two pistols, and the .22 caliber rifles and pistols of the Koenig's kids.

They had also picked up five rifles and four pistols from the Zulu Warriors attack, and those were set aside for the quick reaction forces. The deal with the guards was that the weapons stayed with the position, and the guards switched off the weapons on site as they changed reliefs.

As the bazaar wound down, Richard reflected on how much progress the community had made so far in just a few days, as far as getting organized for survival. By now everyone realized the seriousness of the situation, and it seemed as if a feeling of cooperation and resolve had settled over the residents. After a few hours, he and Sophia had started putting their remaining items back in a box, when suddenly there was a commotion on the other side of the lake near the playground, in front of one of the blanket layouts.

Jacob Hanson yelled at a man named Gary Holmes who was walking away from his blanket, "Hey, give me back my dried fruit."

"What do you mean? This is mine, I traded for this over on the other side of the lake."

Jacob stood up, grabbed Gary by the arm, and said, "That's my writing on the bag, asshole," and then he tried to wrestle the bag away from the thief. They scuffled for a few seconds until Gary punched Jacob in the jaw, and then a real fight began. Before three neighbors were able to separate them, both men were bleeding, Jacob from his mouth and Gary from his nose. Gary also had a cut and swelling lump on his left eye.

Josh was nearby and ran over and yelled to both men, "What the hell is going on?"

Jacob said, "Gary was looking at my stuff, and he palmed a baggie of dried fruit. See, the bag has my writing on it. Look at these other bags I wrote on."

Josh did, and compared the bag Gary had dropped with one from Jacob's layout, then looked at Gary and said, "Gary, what the hell are you doing? That is Jacob's writing so don't try to bullshit me."

Gary looked around, spit on the ground, and said, "Fuck you." Then he pushed his way through the crowd and walked away.

Josh started to go after him, but decide against it. He knew something like this would happen sooner or later, so he just went over to check on Jacob. "Are you OK, Jake?"

"Yeah, Gary has always been an asshole. I'm just pissed that he tried to rip me off. I don't think there is any real damage done to my jaw, but I bit my tongue when he punched me. I'll be sore for a few days, but at least I know that Gary will be hurting a lot more. I got a couple of good quick licks in while his left hand was hanging onto my bag of apricots."

By this time, Richard had made his way over to the scene and Josh told him what had happened. Richard said, "You know, Josh, I had just been thinking how well the bazaar was going, and then this happened. I guess we're lucky there haven't been any conflicts up to now, but you can bet there will be more as things get worse." Richard laid a hand on his brother-in-law's shoulder and said, "Let's give this some thought later on. I've got to help Sophia carry our things back home. Take care, hermano."

As the sky darkened, and evening approached, last trades were made, and all the other families began to pack up their goods and head home. All in all, in spite of the altercation, the bazaar was a big success.

# Chapter 33

There had been little time for the two families to get together since the collapse, but finally the Koenigs had the Cantrells over for dinner that night. Natasha came along as usual- she loved running around playing with the kids in the back yard.

While the kids were occupied outside, the adults enjoyed some cocktails, even though there was no ice. After a nice relaxing chat on how well things were going, considering the circumstances, Carmen and Sophia went out back to heat up some cans of vegetables and spaghetti for supper, using wood in the BBQ grill for heat. For dessert, they had some dried apricots, courtesy of Jacob. It was hardly a feast, but with everyone working so hard, it was a tasty and much needed meal. Both families had freeze dried food in large containers also, but they decided to wait and start integrating those items into their diet slowly as their canned and preserved foods diminished.

Both of the women were on late shift guard duty the next morning, so after putting the kids down for bed, Carmen went to bed and Sophia leashed Natasha and walked home to do the same. Richard and Josh had the night off, so they stayed up and chatted about the future.

"Josh, we've certainly come a log way since Day 1. And so far we've had no serious incidents among the homeowners, but when food starts getting scarce, what do we do when someone steals something from someone else, or there is a fight, or even a shooting among the residents? I think we need to start preparing for the possibility of having to resolve altercations or crimes within the neighborhood. We already have what amounts to a police force with the guard contingent, and later the quick reaction force, but what do we do with thieves or someone who assaults his neighbor? The HOA is non-functioning, and I wouldn't trust them to deal with something as serious as this anyway. We do have that woman former cop in the community. What's her name?"

"You mean Donna Fleer?"

"Yeah, that's her. She knows something about laws and the administration of justice. Maybe we could talk to her, and if she's willing, propose at one of the future meetings that she be elected the Sea Breezes judge, for lack of a better term, and while we're at it, get nominations for residents to be elected as a jury. We could use maybe three trustworthy citizens that are respected and would be impartial and reasonable in determining guilt or innocence in a trial, and to decide on punishment, the ultimate of which would probably be expulsion from the community. What do you think?"

"Sounds good to me, Rich. To tell you the truth, I haven't even thought about that. Why don't you talk to her after the meeting tomorrow and see if she agrees with the concept and is willing to serve? But tonight, let's get out the Sea Breezes roster and map, and organize the four permanent five-person quick reaction force teams. We need to announce the rosters tomorrow and make any adjustments we need before we begin the training sessions later in the morning. If you don't mind, I'll run that, as I've had experience teaching Marine recruits the same tactical skills at the small unit level."

"That makes sense to me, Josh. Let's do the rosters and then I'm going to go home and get some sleep. Sophia and Carmen will be getting up after midnight, and we both need to get some sleep while we can."

They worked on the rosters for about an hour and came up with a rough list of 20 men and women for the quick reaction force teams. They began referring to them as the QRF, since that was less of a mouthful. When they had finished, Richard left the lists with Josh and headed home. He arrived and went to bed in the spare bedroom so as not to wake Sophia, or vice versa when her alarms went off. As he fell asleep, Richard thought of what a remarkable woman he had married, and what a lucky man he was.

# Chapter 34

After the attacks on what was being called everywhere as Day 1, the President of the United States and the White House duty staff had sought refuge in the White House's underground bunker and command center. The President had decided to spend the long weekend catching up on various bills working their way through Congress, and planning new policies to propose.

When the dirty bomb detonated in downtown Washington, D.C., the command center switched to emergency power, and using the hardened and secure communications link to the emergency command centers in the Pentagon, Homeland Security, the FBI, CIA, and other agencies that were always manned 24/7 in case of just such emergencies, the President received the initial confused and spotty situation reports from all agencies and departments.

Since it was a holiday weekend, most of the directors and chiefs, and their staffs, at these agencies and departments were not in their offices, so just about the only people the President had to talk to were duty commanders. Not that that was a big problem, as all of them had been trained extensively to operate in just such emergencies, and the bits of information available began flowing piecemeal into the White House command center.

The President quickly realized how serious things were, and the first order of business that his military aide, the one who carried what is known as "the football" with the nuclear launch codes, recommended, was to contact via secure landline the National Military Command Center, NMCC, in the Pentagon. The NMCC was ordered to contact all U.S. armed forces across the world to put them on a war footing. All military commands were ordered to DEFCON 1, the most severe and ready status, and Permissive Action Links (PAL) communications were verified to all Nuclear Release Authentication System (NRAS) officers in all the command bunkers and headquarters throughout the world.

The PAL codes were the codes needed to unlock nuclear weapons for firing. The NRAS officers were the ones who opened the codes transmitted from the President via the NMCC, and passed them to the firing artillery units, aircraft, and ships. Everything was in order to communicate the release of nuclear weapons to all U.S. operational forces in the world, except, of course, those at Fort Bragg and Fort Hood, which had been paralyzed by the dirty bombs.

Although there were no specific targets yet, based on the lack of any concrete intelligence, the usual suspects, China, North Korea, Iran, and Russia, along with a few others, were specifically targeted. Nuclear attack submarines, called "Boomers," were moved into position within firing range of these countries' major military and civilian centers. At least the U.S. was ready to defend itself from outside invasion, or to retaliate against any country identified as the perpetrator of the attacks.

Speculation was rife among the CIA, FBI, and the rest of the intelligence community about just who was responsible for the attacks, and which country or countries might have been involved. All kinds of theories floated: it was ISIS, coordinating with Russia for the devastatingly debilitating cyber attacks; it was Al Qaeda and China; it was Iran and ISIS. But no one could definitively point a finger at anyone yet. Obviously there was some major world power involved, as the undersea data cables coming into and out of the United States had also been severed. Under the circumstances of a decade-long deterioration of relations with both China and Russia, this would point to one or the other of these nations, but the problem was that it could be any country with a submarine capability, and there were many of them.

The FBI was of little help. They could not identify any overall instigator stateside, although over the few days after the attack, they did point out that known ISIS and Al Qaeda sympathizers in the U.S. took part in the attacks. Enhanced interrogation of those captured was prohibited, so no more details were forthcoming, yet. In a few days, as the situation across a devastated America became known, those prohibitions would be ignored.

With major cities bombed, infrastructure destroyed, nuclear contamination of seven cities and two military bases to deal with, and power and communication out across the U.S., there was neither any real information to impart, nor the means to do it. The President was not used to being told "No," or "We can't," or "I don't know," and was outraged. But it would take several more days to get enough information to even establish an accurate assessment of the situation across America, much less come up with a plan to begin putting transportation, communication, electrical power, and the economy back together.

But by Day 9, the President decided to use the only nation-wide public communication method operational, Ham radio transmissions, to address the American public. At 6 a.m. he recorded the following message, which was transmitted via all Ham radios frequencies:

"My fellow Americans. We have been attacked by cowardly and as yet unknown elements both on the ground and in cyberspace. Although we know that certain extremists, such as Al Qaeda and ISIS, had a hand in these attacks, we do not know who coordinated the attacks, nor do we know who worked with them for the cyber attacks that struck us at the same time. We do not wish war and we will not strike out at any country until we have full, legally verified proof of the guilty organizations or nations.

"Meanwhile, we are working with all government agencies to restore power, communications, transportation, and the economy as quickly as possible. However, due to the massive damage and destruction inflicted on our nation, it will be some time before we can accomplish these difficult tasks.

"We hope to be able to reconstitute and mobilize local National Guard units and deploy active military units as quickly as possible to provide national security within the United States, and eventually local relief. Depending on the areas involved, those that are not contaminated, will eventually see soldiers, food and supplies arrive in their locations as soon as possible, but that will likely be many weeks away, as we must concentrate on the crisis created by the mass evacuations from all of our large cities, as well as deal with cleaning up the contaminated locations.

"It may take awhile to restore power, especially in isolated areas and the cities that were hit with dirty bombs, but rest assured that your government is hard at work in overcoming all obstacles to restore services and security as soon as possible. Until then, I urge all citizens to remain calm, work within your communities to help one another, and trust in your government to come to your rescue.

"You should also know that our allies and friends in Europe have been similarly hit, but because of having to coordinate among the various nations in the European Community, their recovery is expected to take a lot longer. Our military bases in Europe can provide some very limited local help, but they are geared toward readiness and counterstrikes if and when called upon.

"To our enemies, I have a serious warning: Do not think that because America has been weakened that we have lost our resolve, or that we are not capable of immediate retaliation against any nation foolish enough to launch any type of attack against our sovereign territory or overseas installations. Our submarine fleet alone is positioned and capable of destroying any nation on earth, at a moment's notice from me.

"Those of you hearing this message please spread the news among your neighbors and communities. This message will be repeated every hour on the hour for the next three days, and I will have an update for you as soon as I have more information.

"Thank you all, and God Bless America."

# Chapter 35

No one in Sea Breezes was a Ham radio operator, but there were several radios that had receiving capabilities on Ham radio frequencies, and fortunately one of the Sea Breezes residents had been scanning through those frequencies regularly. Donna Fleer woke up at 6:30 a.m., and heard the President's message that was retransmitted a half hour later. She immediately began taking notes of what the President said, and added to them an hour later at the 8 a.m. transmission. Before the 9 o'clock meeting started that morning, she alerted Richard of the message.

Richard began the meeting. "Friends, we have some startling news this morning. Donna has been monitoring Ham radio frequencies and as you know she has been giving updates about news around the rest of the U.S. from Ham operators all across the country. From her reports, we all know that across the U.S., cities and communities are in about the same situation as we are, albeit in isolated country towns, the situation is not as bad, and in those large cities hit by dirty bombs, the situation is much worse."

"That is good to know, but it doesn't make much difference to our community's situation. To our knowledge, there has been no attempt by the government to contact American citizens... until this morning, when Donna heard a message from the President of the United States on a Ham radio frequency."

The homeowners gasped in surprise and anticipation. Richard continued, "Since Donna heard it, I will turn it over to her to tell you what the President had to say."

Donna stood up, and using her notes, gave a very good summary of the President's speech. There was little reaction from the crowd, but the message did offer a small ray of hope for relief arriving to Phelps Island at some time in the future, and that things would, some day, hopefully, start returning to normal.

Donna emphasized that the message was general and nonspecific, especially as far as their immediate situation was concerned. No one had any idea when any help would arrive from the government to their small island off the west coast of Florida. After answering a few questions to repeat certain parts of the President's message, and to give her interpretation, Donna looked over at Richard, smiled, and sat down.

Richard took over and began, "As you all know we have had some occasional attempts by home invaders and small groups to cross the fence into our neighborhood, but, until now, all have been driven away. Of course, no system is perfectly secure, and ours cannot possibly cover every inch of territory. I'm sorry to inform you that sometime very early this morning, two or three men were able to sneak over the fence unseen by the guards, at the Murray home, which is located about halfway between our entrance guard position and the southeast position.

"The home invaders slashed the Murray's screened porch and then broke the glass in the sliding glass door to the living room. Don Murray and his wife and three children were asleep at the time, but Don woke up at the noise of breaking glass, and grabbed his gun. He entered the living room, saw an armed intruder, and shot him several times, killing him.

"He probably was scanning the living room looking for an accomplice, but unknown to him, there was at least one other man in the kitchen. This man shot at Don about five times and hit him twice. Don's wife, Sue, came out in a panic screaming and apparently scared off the other man or men. She had no gun with her so whoever else was involved ran out the back door, vaulted over the fence, and got away. She was lucky they didn't shoot her also. She wasn't sure if there were one or two men, as she ran immediately to Don's side and tried to revive him. Don died in her arms a few minutes later. The entrance guard radioed me and I got there as soon as I could, and some of the Murray's neighbors who heard the shooting had come over to help, and guard the back door.

"There are several lessons we need to learn about this horrible event. First, this emphasizes the need for a quick reaction force in our community. This could have been a larger group instead of a couple of invaders, and if it had been, the whole family, and probably a lot of other neighbors, would have been killed. A lot of the outsiders, including people from Port Monroe, are starting to run out of food, and more and more will become desperate as time goes on. Even normally law-abiding men and women will eventually turn to looting, home invasion, and even killing if they or their children are starving.

"Second, everyone needs to barricade their entrances, especially weakly secured ones such as glass doors and windows, every night. You can use heavy furniture, plywood, or, if you don't have animals or children in your home, booby-traps. I'll talk about those in a minute.

"Third, it would be best if all adults had a gun with them at all times, especially at night. If there are adults without any weapon in their home, see Josh and we'll figure out if we can loan you one- the dead invader had two on him that we can add to the ones we picked up from the Zulus. We won't be able to arm every adult, but we need to do as many as we can, and at least ensure that there is a gun in every house. Please cooperate by telling Josh if you have an extra weapon you can lend out, and contact him if you are an adult and don't have one. The same goes for extra ammunition. Priority will go to the adults who are also on the quick reaction force.

"We're serious here folks. There can be no hoarding of weapons and ammunition, because everyone's security depends on having as many adults as possible armed throughout the community.

"Speaking of the QRF, after this meeting, Josh will read out the names of the morning and afternoon groups, so everyone stick around. If you need to switch from the morning to afternoon, or vice versa, let Josh know and we'll try to work out a swap. Each group will meet in my front yard, and then Josh will lead them through my side and back gates out to the training area.

"I mentioned booby traps earlier so I'll talk about that now before we head off to the first training session. First, please don't put any debilitating traps outside of your home. Warning devices such as a string or wire with cans filled with rocks attached and stretched across your yard at leg level as an audio warning of an intruder are OK, but no punji pits, deadfall traps, or the like. Remember, our quick reaction force especially, not to mention your next-door neighbors, need to be able to move around the entire neighborhood free of danger.

"You can also make several types of injury-producing traps for inside your homes, as long as you don't have kids or animals that could be hurt accidently. For example, you could have a wire across your front and back entrances that you anchor about shin high, so that if anyone is able to get though your door, they will trip themselves, fall, and make a noise.

"You can also get a piece of board or plywood, and nail a bunch of long nails through them, and at night put them down on the floor by entrances, with points up, so an intruder would step on them. In fact, combining both the above would make an invader trip then impale his hands or body on the nails. Both of these traps can be easily picked up and put away in the morning. There are more elaborate traps you can set, and we'll cover those at the training sessions. But use your imagination on what would work in your particular home.

"If there are no questions, I'll turn this over to Josh to read the names of the first and second groups."

Josh read out the names of all four groups and made some adjustments to the groups as necessary. Then he led the first group over to Richard's house.

# Chapter 36

Richard asked Donna to stay after the meeting for something he wanted to get her opinion on, and he led her over to a picnic bench and sat down with her. Donna had a puzzled look on her face, so Richard quickly explained his purpose, broaching the subject about her becoming the Sea Breezes' "Judge."

"Donna, so far we have only had minor scuffles and arguments among our neighbors, but some day that will almost assuredly change, as food runs low, supplies run out, and frustration, depression, and exhaustion start taking their toll on everyone. Josh and I discussed the idea of having an Investigating Judge, of sorts, similar to what some European countries have- someone with legal and courtroom experience to serve as a neutral person to look into crimes such as theft and assaults, and then hold a trial to deal with the perpetrators. We envision you being that person, and we can also appoint or elect three men and women, and maybe an alternate or two, to serve as a jury. We don't have any lawyers in this community, and I think you would be better for this anyway. What do you think?"

Donna pondered the question for a moment and said, "Rich, I understand why you think we need this, and I agree with you. I was about to suggest while you were speaking that you designate a lawyer for the job, but then you pointed out we didn't have any living in Sea Breezes. There are probably a lot of lawyers in Pelican's Landing and and Sunset Beach estates, but that isn't going to help us. So, I'll do it, if the community approves."

"Good, Donna, thanks. How can I help?"

"I'll go home and sit down with a list of all the homeowners and think about who might make good, impartial jurors. I think it would be best to talk to them first to make sure they are willing, and as you say, come up with four or five good citizens who we could propose as candidates for jurors and alternates to the homeowners at a future morning meeting. I don't think we should go through a long drawn out nominating process and debate, since there is just too much to do. Besides, these men and women have to be selected based on their merits and not popularity, although we do need to have a written ballot for the homeowners to vote yes or no, and spaces for write-in candidates.

"I'm thinking about all the details off the cuff now, so let me go home and start to work. I know of a couple of people right off hand whom I would trust to be honest and impartial, and are also easygoing and intelligent, and not likely to be an eventual perpetrator. But even if one is, we'll have an alternate juror or two. Give me until day after tomorrow. We can get together tomorrow night after supper, and I'll show you what I've come up with. We can kick my ideas and names around, and once we agree, I'll present the plan and the names at the morning meeting the day after tomorrow."

"Good, Donna. I would recommend that you leave Josh and me off your list. We already have enough on our plates, and I think our neighbors would be more comfortable with someone who hasn't been telling them what they should do all the time."

Donna smiled, and said, "I agree."

# Chapter 37

Josh herded the first two groups of five adults into the training area he had set up. He first asked if anyone needed any weapons instruction, and three men, including Fred Carlucci and Bill Thornton, and one woman raised their hands. Josh then took the time in front of everyone to go over firearm safety, loading, and aiming procedures. He then told the four who had never fired a weapon that they would get some live firing practice at the end of the session.

Josh went though some basic drills on fire and movement, taking cover, and the difference between concealment (not being able to be seen) and cover (being protected from enemy fire). He split each five-person team into two smaller "fire teams" of two persons each, and assigned the fifth person as the overall commander of the force. He then pulled out a Sea Breezes map and designated an initial rallying point landmark for each group, since their homes were all near each other. From the rallying point, it was a matter of getting everyone assembled, moving to the sound of gunfire, scoping out the situation, deploying, and firing at the intruders. They would probably need to maneuver, and maybe even split up the two fire teams, and that was why there was an overall commander.

Josh also reminded each group that they had no communications, and that whichever team was scheduled for duty on that day's rotation, each team member was responsible for reacting as soon as they heard gunfire, assembling quickly at the rallying point, and then moving to contact under the direction of the team commander. It was far from an ideal plan, but it was the best they could do.

He told the team commanders to get together with their group and practice forming up at their designated rallying point at a pre-designated time once in awhile, moving to an attack location, and practice "assaulting" any attackers. He left it to each QRF team to decide when to do it, and where in the neighborhood to launch their pretend assault, but told them not to do it at night. The guards on the rooftops didn't need a bunch of unidentified guys with guns running around the streets.

They practiced everything, and then let the fire team leaders practice with their fire teams, one man shooting while the other moved, advancing in short hops, and other maneuvers, as he watched and critiqued. By lunchtime, he had done all he could, and told everyone but the new shooters to go home.

Josh had set up some simple silhouette targets and had brought an extra rifle, shotgun, and pistol so that each individual could fire not only the type of weapon he or she carried, but also one of each of the other types of firearm.

They spent about 30 minutes firing, and as it turned out, Bill was a pretty good shot. Josh noted that Bill took some pride at having been the most accurate shooter of the group, and thought again of how useful the guy had been and what an asset he was to the community.

Fred and the woman were rather hopeless, as they could not overcome their fear of guns. But eventually both were able to at least get a bullet in the silhouette somewhere, and that was good enough.

The training process was repeated with the next two five-person teams that afternoon, and at the end of the second session, Josh was pretty satisfied with the day's weapons and movement training. After suffering several attacks, the men and women of Sea Breezes had gotten serious about their need for protection, and all were if not eager, at least resigned to their new duties as fighters.

In the event of an attack, Josh and Richard would also run to the sound of gunfire and assess the situation to see if another group, or even all of them, was needed for call-up. Whichever one of them arrived at the scene first would assume overall command, and the other would serve as a messenger to run and alert other groups as needed.

All in all, it was a pretty good day, and Josh stayed at Richard's house to discuss the day's training. Sophia brought them each a not-so-cold beer, and they filled her in on what they had accomplished that day. Josh said that all in all, the training had gone as well as they could have expected.

# Chapter 38

At the next 9 a.m. meeting one of the recent widows, who also had three children, stood up and said, "My name is Ana Serrano, and I'm starting to run out of food. I've been careful and rationed what I had, but we didn't have much on hand on Day 1, and although I really appreciate what the scavenging parties have shared with us, we're getting low, down to maybe enough for three or four more days. We can get by without real toilet paper, and other niceties, but now I just don't know what to do. And, it hasn't rained in awhile and I'm almost out of water too. I'm alone and I'm starting to get desperate." By the time she was through, there were tears running down her cheeks.

Richard looked around and saw several others nodding their heads. He thought a minute and said, "Look, obviously, some of us either by luck or planning, had a good supply of food on hand when the lights went out. But it's also obvious we're not going to find much of anything left at the shopping centers or convenience stores so...."

Richard was interrupted by another woman who introduced herself as Marie Atkins, who said, "Maybe there is one more source of food we could check out. At the church where we used to have our HOA meetings, I remember seeing signs about collecting donations to establish a food bank for the needy, and I'm pretty sure the collection date was before the attacks hit. Maybe there is something there we could find if they didn't already hand out the donated food. And let's face it, a lot of us now certainly qualify as needy."

Richard smiled and said, "Great idea, Marie. We'll get a group of four or five cars and head over there after lunch at one o'clock.

"But what I was also going to say is that if you remember, last week I said how important it was to keep our lake free of pollution, and all winter we have all seen geese fly in from the north and hang around for a few days, plus we have our normal contingent of resident ducks. There are also a lot of squirrels running around our trees, and I think it's time to set up some hunting parties and schedule some hunts. I don't want everyone to go blasting away at random and make our security guards nervous or confused, or to create a hazardous situation and put people at risk of getting hit by a stray bullet, so Josh and I will organize a couple of hunting teams, one for shooting some of the birds in the lake, and one for the squirrels in the trees, and brief them on safe shooting procedures.

"We can also head out across the open field behind my house and into the forest and swamps to see if there are any deer, possum, or other animals we can find. We'll let the guards on duty know when and where the hunting parties go out so that we don't create any confusion or alarm."

Several people nodded their heads in agreement. Then Bill Thornton stood up and said, "I don't have a lot to do now, as the wounded we had in the aid station have recovered enough to go back to their homes. I got to thinking that although the HOA's rules prohibit fishing in our lake, we can certainly do that under these circumstances, and maybe even put together a fishing team that goes out under protection and fishes from the marsh area... maybe even get close enough to do a little fishing from the gulf shore."

"There are no homes between us and the woods and marsh to our north, east and west, and I haven't seen anyone around the field we were training in. I did some fishing in my free time before the crisis hit, and I taught my kids how also. We have some gear and I bet there are some other fisherman among us."

Richard said, "Another great idea, Bill. After the meeting, anyone who fishes or has fishing gear, please stick around and talk to Bill. Any hunters, or anyone who wants to try their hand at hunting, see Josh after the meeting. You two can coordinate your schedules so that only one group is out at a time."

"From those of you remaining who have cars with gas, please see me after lunch, and I'll organize a group to head over to the Church and see what we can find.

"One last thing on the food. For folks who are almost out of food, like Ana, stick around and meet with Sophia. Sophia, raise your hand."

Sophia stood up and waved and said, "Anyone in real need of food, meet me over by the swings after the meeting. Carmen and I have some food we can share and if anyone else has some they can spare, meet us over there also. Please be honest about your need, and compassionate if you can help out a hungry neighbor."

Richard continued, "Now as far as the last thing Ana mentioned, water, I can solve that easily. I have a well and a pump I use to connect well water to the irrigation system for my yard, and when I had it installed, I had the contractor put in a valve that I could switch over so the water runs out of a normal outdoor-type faucet instead of through the irrigation system. It comes in handy for washing cars or spot watering without having to pay extra on my water bill.

"I'll hook my hose up and anyone who needs water should gather up all the containers you can find. Bring your whole family to help carry all the full ones back home, and come by my house at 10:30 to fill up. Anyone who has battery chargers, or anything that needs to be charged, bring them before 10:30 and I'll hook them up and charge them for as long as the generator is running. I'll keep the pump and generator running until everyone has gotten all they can carry. I'm sure a few other neighbors have the same setup, so please raise your hands and shout out your name and address if you do."

Two others did so, and Richard said, "Thanks. We'll work up some kind of once a week schedule for rotating water pumping locations later. Hopefully, we won't have many more unusual dry spells though.

"OK, friends, this has been a really productive meeting, and we have several groups that need to meet. Any questions before we break up? OK, let's get going, and I'll see all of you here tomorrow morning."

# Chapter 39

After lunch, Richard had gotten eleven other men and two women together for the scavenging hunt, and one of the women had suggested they also check the Catholic church on the other side of Beach Parkway. "It's not near any stores, and maybe no one has thought to look there. We could search our Baptist church first, and then head on over to the other one. It's not that far away and with plenty of guys with rifles hanging out of windows and the bed of pickups, the trip should be pretty safe."

Everyone agreed, and five cars and trucks were selected to go with all fourteen people, each armed with either a rifle, shotgun or pistol, and some had both a long gun and a handgun. They decided that when they arrived, five people would stay with the cars, and watch them and the road; four would surround the church and secure the outside, two would enter and clear the church to make sure it was unoccupied, then guard the front and back doors. Once they gave the all clear, the remaining three, including Josh, would search the premises, starting in the basement.

In the Baptist church basement they found a locked storeroom, which Josh blew open with a single shotgun slug to the simple lock. Sure enough, inside they found one wall with shelves that had 30 or so boxes of canned and packaged food from the food drive a few weeks ago.

They quickly loaded all of these into the cars and trucks. They continued searching, but found only a couple of cans of sugar, powdered cream, and coffee in another room that looked like a break room. Inside the refrigerator, there was some spoiled food, but also a couple of cases of warm soft drinks, which they also loaded up. Once they had everyone back in the cars, they took off for the Catholic church.

On the way over, along Beach Parkway, they were passed by two cars that were apparently heading for the bridge to Port Monroe. The cars were filled with Black men who eyed them as they passed, but they didn't pull any weapons on the heavily armed convoy, and accelerated on past them. They also passed a man on a motorcycle wearing a black leather jacket, on the back of which was a drawing of a snarling wolf and the word "Werewolves." Richard noted the AR-15 slung across his back. The rider also briefly eyed the convoy, but he accelerated his bike and rode away quickly.

They arrived at the Catholic church a few minutes later, and performed the same procedure they had done back at the Baptist church. In this church, all they found were some more sugar and coffee, and a dozen or so cases of soft drinks stacked up in a small storeroom. They loaded these items into the vehicles and headed home.

The trip to the Catholic church hadn't yielded all that much in supplies, but it was worth the trip, not just for the few items they found, but also for the intelligence gathered. Now they knew that there was at least one other group out there besides the Zulu Warriors that was doing some reconnoitering around the island. They stopped at the Koenig's house and Carmen and Josh helped them unload everything into their dining room and den, to store until the next morning's meeting.

Richard asked those men and women who ventured out on the trip to pass around the word of their success, so that everyone would show up at the next morning's meeting. They could parcel out the food and drinks after it was over. Richard said he'd coordinate with Sophia and Carmen to see which families were in dire need, and set aside extra for them.

# Chapter 40

Richard and Sophia, and of course, Natasha, spent another evening with the Koenigs. It was much easier for them to travel than it was for the Koenigs and their kids to make the trip to the Cantrells' house.

Over a dwindling supply of Jack Daniels, the adults talked about the day's events. Richard described the partial success of the churches scavenging hunt, and added the sighting of what Richard presumed was a reconnaissance by the Zulu Warriors and the Werewolves, since both sightings were very obviously not out for a planned daylight raid. Still it worried all of them. Josh made a note to alert the quick reaction force commanders at the next morning's meeting.

Sophia brought up the subject of the food-distressed families. The meeting had identified four families that needed food within the next few days, and she was pleased that in addition to the Koenigs and the Cantrells, three other family representatives volunteered some of their food to help the needy. She said that two of them had indicated that they had, like the Koenigs and the Cantrells, prepared for a possible disaster by accumulating some preserved and freeze-dried food.

They had also discussed the moral obligation to help their unprepared neighbors versus the need for taking care of their own families. The latter of course had priority, but all acknowledged that on a practical level, they also needed everyone in the community healthy enough to contribute to the security and other common community tasks. One of the neighbors with extra food was a Mormon who had, as was recommended by his Church, a year's supply of food for his family, and he had offered to contribute over half of it to the community's needy. That was extremely generous and would go a long way to help alleviate current shortages.

Josh then talked about the hunting and fishing parties. Bill Thornton's fishing would begin at dawn tomorrow with six people around the lake, and there would be a 10-fish of any size limit per person so as not to deplete the lake's fish population. Hopefully, there would be some fish to add to the scavenged and shared food to be distributed at the meeting.

Josh also said that they had put together one group of six hunters for squirrel and other small animals that lived in the housing area. Possum, raccoons, and even armadillos had been sighted in the neighborhood, and although not all that palatable, they would still provide nutrition. The guards had been notified that they would be out hunting at dawn the next day.

Sophia made sure that they knew the various degrees of severity of the food shortages of the four families in food crisis so that extra portions of everything handed out tomorrow would go to them. Richard asked her for a list of each of the four families' food supply levels so he could balance the extra rations for each according to how bad off they were.

Another group of "outside" hunters were designated, along with two security guards for the hunting party. They would assemble in Richard's front yard and head out his back gate to begin their hunt at dawn.

Carmen and Sophia got up to begin preparations for cooking a meager supper on the BBQ grill while Richard and Josh hashed out the logistics of gathering and distributing all the food from various sources at the next morning's meeting. Richard and Carmen had second shift guard duty to perform so there was no prolonged chat after they had eaten.

After supper, Richard decided to stop by Donna's house on the way home to discuss the juror list she had made up. She invited the couple and Natasha in, and started laying out her ideas. Donna informed him that the word had gotten out and that Fred Carlucci had dropped by and insisted that his name be on the ballot for judge. Richard agreed with Donna that it was probably a good idea to add him, and just hope for the best. He quickly became aware that Donna had done her homework on searching out qualified jurors and preparing the ballots, and the meeting with her lasted less than 10 minutes. The Cantrells said their goodbyes, and walked home.

Richard and Sophia, headed for their bedroom, and Richard set an alarm for his guard duty. Then they both fell asleep on the bed, spooning together, in exhaustion. That night there were no security events.

# Chapter 41

After Richard had returned from his guard duty shift, he woke Sophia at 8 the next morning for breakfast, and as they were conversing, she suggested to Richard that they needed to coordinate the guard duty schedule so that childless couples were together on the same shift and then off at the same time, as well as arranging schedules for couples with children so as to leave at least a full night each week for some time together with their families.

"I know that this will be difficult to coordinate, since everyone is pulling both day and night shifts now, but if we don't, the stress from being apart most of the time could eventually adversely affect morale. Carmen even brought up to me that she and the kids rarely saw Josh because he was always so busy working on community issues."

Richard realized that he too had been preoccupied with organizing the defense and provision of the Sea Breezes community, at the expense of his marriage. Frankly, he missed being with Sophia, and decided to do something about it.

Richard told Sophia that he would talk to Josh about arranging schedules to give couples and families some time together once or twice a week. He knew that that would complicate Josh's scheduling problem, but he also agreed that it was necessary. He smiled and gave her a long kiss before he walked out the door so he could catch Josh before the morning meeting.

Knowing that some food was going to be distributed, almost all the adult residents who weren't on guard duty showed up at the meeting. Carmen and Josh had gotten up early and divided up all the food, soft drinks, and bottled water and placed them in garbage bags. Plastic bags were irreplaceable now, and got a lot of repeated use until they tore. They had also filled up four boxes of food for those families in real need.

Josh began the 9 a.m. meeting telling everyone of the hunting and fishing plans, and added that that morning, the fisherman had caught 43 fish, and the hunters had bagged eight squirrels and four possums, plus eleven geese and five ducks, after the fishing had been completed. They could have killed more ducks, but they didn't want to completely deplete their local duck population. The geese were transients, so they killed all they could as they were sitting in the lake, to add to the food supplies to be distributed after the meeting. The crowd of neighbors cheered at the good news- it would be a welcome change to have some fresh meat on their tables again to supplement their limited diet.

Richard stood up and said, "Most of you know about the success of our scavenging trips to the churches, and the food and drinks we were able to gather. Several of us have also chipped in some of our stock of preserved food, and we also have some meat and fish, thanks to the hunters and fishermen. Everything will be distributed after the meeting, and those families in need will get an extra portion. Sorry, folks, but you have to clean and smoke your own fish and squirrels."

This got a little chuckle from the crowd, so Richard continued, "Also I'm announcing another Sea Breezes Bazaar for tomorrow after lunch so that all families can swap food, goods and services to balance out their needs again."

"But before we do that I want to bring up an important subject that we need to discuss. Donna, I'll turn this over to you."

Donna got up and explained the substance of the earlier discussion with Richard on the need for some type of system to resolve issues of community confrontations that went beyond the level of scuffles and arguments, as well as more serious infractions.

"In addition to some type of judicial process, I have also thought about the need for mediation of problems that don't rise to the level of crimes. I think that is where we most need a mediator and juror panel now, but we need to decide who will be, for lack of a better term, the judge and jurors for both mediation and criminal acts.

"There haven't been any major incidents yet, but with hunger, fatigue, and stress setting in, we are bound to need some way of dealing with problems that come up. Richard has suggested to me that I run for the position of judge, based on my police experience, and Fred Carlucci has added his name to the ballot based on his experience as the HOA president. I have also made up a list of five jurors and alternates to serve on any mediation meeting or criminal trial that might arise in the future.

"I have made up ballots to hand out to every family, and they contain my name and Fred Carlucci's for judge, and the five mediator/jurors that I believe are qualified, and who have volunteered to be jurors. Beside each juror's name is also a yes or no block to check, and there is also a write-in line for both the judge and juror selections.

"Please mark your ballots and bring them to Josh's bench under the covered picnic area at tomorrow morning's meeting. Make sure one adult from each household signs his or her name, and drop it in the box beside Josh on your way in. He will count the ballots and announce the results at the end of the meeting tomorrow."

Then it was Josh's turn to explain that he would be adjusting the guard duty schedules to allow couples at least one full night off together each week. He also said he would make sure that singles who had hooked up with other singles had the same opportunity, but he needed for them to drop by his house after the meeting so he could add their names in private, if they wished.

As it turned out, there were two more couples who signed up on that list, and Josh was surprised that Jacob Hanson, who had fought with Gary Holmes after Gary had tried to steal from him, had hooked up with Ana Serrano- she who made the statement at the meeting about her and her children running out of food. Ana was a nice-looking woman, and Jacob was a bachelor. Josh suspected that the liaison may have had more of an "economic" than romantic motive on the part of Ana; but who was he to judge?

Sophia and Carmen were up next, and announced that they were ready to distribute the supplies they had accumulated. They had arranged equal piles of food, and called the names of the four families most in need first. Carmen reminded everyone that if they were not satisfied with the items they were allocated, they had the opportunity to exchange and barter for preferred items at the next afternoon's bazaar.

One adult per family lined up, and their names were checked off a roster of the homeowners as they came forward. The food distribution was orderly, and the heads of families filed by to receive a few cans or boxes of food, sodas, and either fresh fish or meat, that comprised their equal per person shares.

The rest of the day was spent by the homeowners tending to their chores, getting water, cleaning the fish, birds and animals, and resting. There were no security incidents that night.

# Chapter 42

At the 9 a.m. meeting, after all the ballots for the "judge" and "jurors" had been cast, the subject was brought up about the three homes whose owners had left for the long weekend when the attacks occurred, and hadn't returned home. Everyone listened to varying arguments that these folks probably wouldn't be returning, and that the community should go ahead and break into the houses and scavenge food and supplies. There were many people who objected to "robbing their absent neighbors," but in the end, those who favored doing so won out.

Richard took a vote and the community decided to send in a team to the three houses to gather food and other useful items, with the caveat that when or if any family returned, they would be fully compensated. A list of items and food taken would be made and kept by whoever was elected as judge.

Richard then announced that the outside hunters had limited success in that morning's dawn outing, bagging a few birds of various types, some possum, and some feral dogs. The latter were killed in self defense, as the dogs, smelling the blood of the hunter's kills, attacked them. They were originally inclined to leave the dogs, but after considering that other cultures ate dogs as a delicacy, decided to bring them back and butcher them. The fishermen had ventured out to the gulf beach, and landed various forms of sea creatures, including fish and crabs. All of this food was taken back, dressed, butchered, cleaned, and cut into small strips and smoked.

He encouraged everyone to come to the bazaar, because the meat plus the items from the three unoccupied homes would be distributed at the same time. That would mean only a handful of meat and maybe one or two cans or packages of food... better than nothing, though.

Sophia had counted the votes while the discussions were going on, and she ended the meeting by announcing the election results. Donna had been elected over Fred as the Sea Breezes' Judge (and by a wide margin, although Sophia didn't mention that), and of the five jurors nominated, four were elected along with one write-in, Jacob Holmes. Apparently the homeowners respected a man who had stood up and fought to defend his property.

Josh headed up a team of two men and one woman to check out the three empty houses. They found a normal amount of food and supplies in two of the houses, but one had already been raided. It just happened to be next door to the thief, Gary Holmes' house, but of course no one could prove that he had been the perpetrator.

The second bazaar was of limited success. Richard had noted that a lot of the neighborhood's trees had been drastically trimmed, which explained the large amount of firewood for trade. Other than that, most of the families were just trading items they didn't want or need, for items they needed or wanted more.

But everyone appreciated the distribution of the meat and items salvaged from two of the empty homes at the beginning of the bazaar. It was another successful, although much smaller, event than the first one, and everyone went home afterwards to their afternoon routines.

Both Richard and Sophia had the entire night off. The uneventful day finally allowed them some much-needed downtime together. Richard took the opportunity to lie down on the couch with Sophia and just hold her in his arms. After a long and comfortable period of just being close to his beautiful wife, relaxing and talking about mundane things, he rose and suggested they both take a "bath," which consisted of a bucket of warm water, a wash rag, and a small bar of soap. They bathed each other slowly and toweled themselves dry. Sophia led Richard to their bedroom, lit a candle on the nightstand, and drew him down on the bed beside her. It was a great way to end the day.

# Chapter 43

At the 9 a.m. meeting, there was little to discuss, except another reminder to gather and conserve water, but to leave the lake water alone. Josh also reminded everyone to keep building up their home barricades and conserve their food.

Home gardens were discussed, and everyone was encouraged to clear out part of their back yards and start planting the seeds from the ACE hardware store that had been distributed. This was backbreaking work, and most of the residents spent the day working on their gardens. One homeowner who already had a back yard garden also had a gas powered tiller, which he loaned out to other folks who needed to dig up part of their back lawns. All in all, it was a quiet day.

But that night, disaster struck.

## Chapter 44

Since there was no electricity, the community's fires and candles usually went out at night, and by 8 p.m., most of the residents had gone to bed, and were asleep by 8:30 or 9. The guards had been posted at dusk, and were obviously not as alert as they should have been when the attack began just before midnight.

It began not at the main entrance or along Connor Drive, but along the back, or northern, side of the community, by a force of 25 or 30 armed gang members climbing over the north fence into the back yards of several homes on both the northeast and northwest corners. They had come through the woods on the east and west sides of the community, probably having parked out of earshot on Connor Drive.

The guard post near the northeast corner spotted the attackers as they were climbing over the fence, and opened fire, but the guard on the northwest corner had either fallen asleep or did not notice the infiltration until they broke into a home and started shooting.

The QRF team that was on duty responded to the gunfire, joined up and moved out in about seven minutes. They headed to the northeast side, since that was where the gunfire was first heard. It was a decent turnout of four out of the five men and women that comprised the QRF team up first for duty that night.

The situation was confusing, because the attacking force had crossed the fence in at least two locations in the northeast. The force commander, who happened to be Donna Fleer that night, took charge of her team.

"OK, it looks like there are only going to be four of us tonight. We'll split up into two fire teams of two people each: Ed, you're with me. Louise and Mike, you're the second team. There's a lot of shooting going on, so this must be a pretty large attack. As we get close to the shooting, Louise, you and Mike move to the left flank of the firing and we'll move to the right. Stay low and covered, and advance slowly. If you see a clear target, shoot, and keep shooting until you hit all the attackers you see. Watch for muzzle flashes in case the bad guys are hidden."

There was no firing from the front yards of the homes, so they closed in and began firing at figures visible on the sides of the houses, as well as those between the fence and the house. Donna's team had actually practiced this maneuver and the attackers in the back yards were caught in their crossfire.

After his initial shots, the guard on the roof had been keeping his head down, as he was overwhelmed by the firing of the many attackers from the other side of the fence. But he got some relief from the homeowners around him who had gone to their windows and started firing also. When he realized that the QRF team had arrived and was keeping the attackers from advancing and shooting, he began firing again. The attacking force only managed to get inside one home, and they killed the homeowner, but his wife was also armed and she shot one man, driving the rest out of her house into the back yard.

None of the adjacent homes had been breached, and when the attackers realized they were taking a lot of fire from the ground on their flanks, they all retreated into the back yard, wondering what to do. After some frantic firing at the homeowners to keep their heads down, the attackers who had not been killed or disabled retreated back over the fence.

Remarkably, no one on Donna's QRF team was hit, as their assault on the flanks had thoroughly surprised and confused the attacking force. The roof top guard kept firing at the attackers as they retreated, wounding at least two of them. Once the enemy had escaped, Donna made a quick decision.

Hyped up with adrenaline and almost out of breath, she shouted, "Louise, you and Mike stay here and secure the bodies of the fallen attackers; if there are any that are just wounded, disarm them, tie them up good and leave them against the fence where the guard on the roof can see them. Then get up on the roof with the guard and watch to make sure they don't come back."

Louise said, "What about the wounded homeowners? Shouldn't we help them?"

"Not now. Let the homeowners deal with them. You guys need to get up there and provide security. Ed, come with me. We're going out the back gate and see what's going on over on the northwest side. I hear more firing over there."

Donna and Ed took off, and Louise and Mike started checking out the fallen attackers. One of the wounded was foolish enough to go for a gun in his waistband as Ed was checking him out. Louise shot him twice, and he was still.

Richard had awakened as the first shots were being fired nearby, and he jumped out of bed, grabbed his Bersa, and seeing no one in his back yard headed outside in his shorts, followed by Natasha. He briefly thought to himself that it was a good thing he had locked the gate to the empty field behind his house. He noticed a man climbing over his neighbor's fence two houses down, and opened fire on him, hitting him with at least one of his shots, but he had to hit the ground when an attacker who had already crossed over into the same yard began returning fire.

Inside the house, Sophia grabbed the walkie-talkie and radioed Josh, "Hello, Josh. This is Sophia, come in."

It only took a few seconds for Josh to get to his radio, and respond, "This is Josh, Sophia, what's going on? I hear firing from over near where you are."

"It sounds like we're being attacked on the northeast corner. I don't know where the QRF team is, but Richard said you'd better call out the standby QRF team in case we're attacked from other locations."

"OK, I will, and I'd better alert all the other QRF teams to stand by, just in case. Shit, this is bad. Where's Rich?"

"He's out back and I saw him firing towards the east. There's a lot of gunfire over in that direction."

"Yeah, I hear it. That's probably the first QRF team arriving. I'm also hearing shots on the northwest corner too. I'll get the standby team out and rolling in that direction. Tell Richard to call me in five minutes or so while I round them up."

"OK, will do. Hurry, Josh." Sophia dropped the radio on the couch, ran and got their shotgun, and waited in the hallway, watching the front and back doors.

As Richard was crouching low on the ground due to the incoming fire, a man crossed the Cantrell's fence behind him. But as soon as his feet hit the ground, a 60-pound flash of black and white fur knocked him down. Natasha clamped her jaws on the man's left forearm and wouldn't let go. Richard heard the snarling, and a shot, rolled over on his back, and started rapid firing at the intruder's upper torso until he fell.

Natasha lay next to the body, whimpering. She had been shot in her right thigh and was bleeding steadily. Richard ran over and picked her up and ran into the house. Sophia lowered the shotgun she had pointed at the back door, and breathed a sigh of relief when she saw Richard, but ran over to him with a cry when she saw him carrying Natasha, her leg covered in blood.

"Oh my God, Rich, are you OK? Were you hit? Is Tasha OK?"

Richard was breathing hard, but managed a few short sentences between breaths, "No, I wasn't hit. Tasha saved me, but she was shot. Get me a flashlight."

Richard laid Natasha down on the carpet in the living room, and Sophia grabbed a flashlight and shined it on Natasha's leg. Natasha whined in pain as Sophia examined her wound while Richard held her down.

He said, "She was hit in the thigh, but it doesn't look like the bone was broken. I think she'll be all right. Clean up her wound and put a compress on the entry and exit holes, and bandage her leg tightly to stop the bleeding."

As she worked, Sophia told him about calling Josh to get reinforcements out. Richard leaned back against the couch and caught his breath as he listened.

"Rich, Josh wants you to call him in a few minutes He's rounding up the standby QRF team and probably heading to the northwest corner." She stifled a sob and added, "Everything's so confusing."

"Don't worry, Hon. We're reacting well. I'm going to check out back. You keep Tasha calm. Don't let her try to get up. Here, take the Bersa and watch both doors. If the area out back and over the fence is all clear, I'll call Josh back and see where he's going, then I'm going to go and try to meet up with him and the second QRF team. Be careful. I love you."

Richard gave her a quick kiss, grabbed the radio, the shotgun and a bandoleer of shells, and eased out the back door in a crouch, scanning left and right. He looked both ways across the fences to his neighbors' yards and the empty field, but couldn't see anyone. Apparently between him and Natasha, and the homeowner from where Richard was being shot at, they had eliminated the attackers nearby. He hollered at the homeowners on either side who were also out in their back yards to keep a look out. He pulled out the walkie-talkie and called Josh.

"Josh, this is Rich. Listen we've been hit along our northern perimeter but the firing now seems to be concentrated around the northwest corner. I think the QRF team on duty took care of the northeast area where I first heard firing- it's quiet over there now. If there were any more attackers moving around over there, someone would be shooting."

"Rich, I got the second QRF team mobilizing, and I'm heading up to the lake now. It looks like they're only three of them though. They must be waiting for two more guys. I'll meet up with you at the lake area. See you when you get here. I think we'd better head up to the northwest corner ASAP." He pocketed the radio and ran up to join the three men already assembled.

Richard went through his side gate out to the front, and jogged toward the lake area in time to catch Josh and the second QRF moving down Flagler Road towards the firing.

Josh had checked his duty roster and notified the nearest member of the standby QRF team to alert their team and meet up at the lake. Unfortunately, it took longer than it should have because the team commander lived in the northwest area and couldn't be reached- he was probably involved in the firefight. Only three men responded, and when Josh was told about not being able to get to the team commander, he took command of the team in the absence of their regular leader. Richard arrived just as they started to move out to the area under siege, and joined them.

Since the attackers had the advantage of surprise on this side of their two-pronged attack, thanks to a drowsy guard, they were able to get inside four homes and control them. They killed several of the homeowners and began to loot their homes, including capturing two women and one teenage girl, forcing them over the back fence. Six of the attackers had set up security around the four homes, three on each side, in accordance with their attack plan, while their comrades emptied the houses of food, weapons, and the women.

The guard on the roof didn't wake up until he heard the sounds of the first shots inside the houses, but he managed to fire a few rounds and hit one of the last men coming over the fence before he had to duck down from return fire. The two security teams of the attackers were confused for a few minutes until they realized where the fire was coming from. They lay low until the roof top guard was engaged and had to crouch down away from the incoming fire. Then they started scanning around looking for targets.

When Richard, Josh, and the three members from the second QRF were getting close to the firing, Richard said, "Josh, if you give me one man I'll head through the back yards and move around to the right side. If you can do the same with your two on the left, we can probably surprise them".

Josh nodded, "OK. Leroy, Chad, come with me. Cameron, you go with Rich. Everyone, be careful you don't shoot each other. Spread out at least five yards apart and open fire as soon as you see the attackers."

As the teams split up, Josh led his men out of the street and to the left, keeping close to the front of the houses as he slowly and carefully approached the houses under siege. The two QRF fire teams knew the general area where the attackers were located because of the sporadic firing of the roof top guard and the return fire, but before they could head down the side of a house to get into the back yard, they were surprised by the security guards. Two of them opened fire, and Chad was hit twice in the chest and fell backwards, dead before he hit the ground. Josh had his upper arm grazed by a bullet but it was not serious and it didn't slow him down.

He dropped to the ground and started returning fire, aiming at the muzzle flashes. Leroy had hit the ground as soon as the firing began, his quick reaction drilled into him by many similar situations during his tour in Viet Nam. He used Richard's return fire as cover to crawl over behind a big oak tree. He got into position and returned fire also, killing one of the attackers' security guards.

After the two teams split up, Richard and Cameron had made their way along the right side of Flagler Road, and into the back yards of the houses, moving from back yard to back yard, until he was past the houses facing the street from where the attackers were firing. He suddenly was afraid that one of the homeowners might shoot at them, but fortunately they were looking out their front windows at the houses under siege across the street, searching for targets.

After passing the area where the shots were coming from, Richard and Cameron turned up along the side of a house, no more than 20 yards from the security guards stationed on the right side. They were not noticed by the enemy, who were being distracted by the firing on Josh and Leroy's side. Richard crouched down and fired his shotgun at the security team, hitting one of the men in the face with double aught buckshot.

Cameron had come up along the side of a house behind Richard, and as Richard fired, Cameron tried to move to cover behind a tree, but instead of crawling he tried to run. One of the security guards fired and shot his leg out from under him. Richard cursed, and fired again at the two security guards still in action.

"Cameron, stay low and crawl on over behind the tree now! I'm covering you. Get moving!"

Richard had loaded one round in the chamber and had a five-round magazine on his semi-auto 12 gauge. He rapid fired three more rounds, and just as his five-round magazine emptied and the bolt locked back, Cameron reached the big oak tree and and pulled himself behind it a second or two before the guards fired at him, the rounds thumping into the tree trunk.

Richard had to take cover as he ejected the shotgun's magazine. He rolled behind the corner of the house and rammed in another five-round magazine and let the bolt go forward, chambering a round. He waited for a few seconds but didn't hear any more firing. He fired two more times at the guards' positions, just to be sure, but got no return fire. This time he waited a few minutes, but couldn't see anyone, so he fired another round, and ran over to the oak tree behind Cameron. No one shot at him. He made a quick check of Cameron's wound, and saw it wasn't too bad.

"You OK, Cameron?"

"Yeah. I saw two guys run around to the back a minute ago so I think they've given up and are running."

"OK, let's wait a few minutes more just to make sure. Keep your eyes peeled."

Of the enemy security guards protecting the looting of the homes, three were shot and killed, and the other three, one of whom was wounded, decided to pull back, since their comrades had finished cleaning out the homes, and they had been taking more fire than they had bargained for. They had fired a couple of parting shots at both Josh and Richard, then took off running back towards the fence. On his side of the security guards, Leroy was the only one to get a couple of shots off at them as they ran, but he didn't think he hit anyone.

After a few minutes, since Richard hadn't heard any firing from Josh's side for a while either, he hollered over to Josh, "Josh, everything clear on your side?"

Josh hollered back, "All clear over here."

"Josh, have your guys cover you- Cameron will cover me. Let's meet in between."

When they were face to face, Richard asked, "Are your guys OK?"

"No, we lost Chad. He took two rounds and must have died in seconds."

"Aw, Jesus. He was my next-door neighbor and a good guy. Anyone else?"

"I was clipped on the arm but it's nothing serious. It just broke the skin and left a furrow on my biceps. It'll make a nice scar. You guys OK?"

"Cameron was hit in the leg but I think he'll be OK- it didn't look like the bullet hit a bone, but he's in a lot of pain. And I guess the gods of war figured I had enough scars. Let me look at your arm."

"No, it's OK, really. It's already stopped bleeding. I'll go see Julia later and get her to put a bandage on it after she's taken care of all the other wounded. Let's check out the guys we shot."

While Josh and Richard's fire teams had been engaging the security guards, Donna had taken Ed out the back gate of Sea Breezes Drive and slowly moved west along the fence toward the shooting. When she saw the attackers start crossing back over the fence and begin fleeing into the woods, she and Ed hit the ground and started firing at them as fast as they could pull the triggers, downing several more attackers. When there was no more firing for a few minutes, she moved in a crouch slowly towards the northwest corner, and as she was approaching she yelled as loud as she could, "Hey! It's Donna and Ed! Don't shoot! We're coming over the fence!" She kept up the chatter to make sure everyone on the other side knew they were friendlies, "It's Donna and Ed. Don't shoot. We're coming over. Don't shoot. Don't shoot."

As she climbed over and dropped down to the ground she met Richard who grinned at her and said, "OK, Donna, I didn't shoot. What were you doing over on the other side of the fence?"

Donna related what had happened with her QRF team from the time they had first deployed until the shooting stopped on the northeast side. She went on to tell him what she and Ed had done, and how they, along with the roof guard, had shot at the fleeing attackers.

Richard smiled and said, "Great thinking Donna. You must have hurt them bad. Better get on back to your team and check up on them and your prisoners. Have the homeowners help any of the wounded back to the aid station. Your team had better stay on alert until dawn in case they decide to come back."

Richard, Josh, and Leroy started checking on the attackers who were either dead or wounded and disarmed them all. They tied up the wounded and dragged them over to the back fence. He turned to Leroy and Josh and said, "Guys, I'll help the homeowners evacuate our wounded back to the aid station. Why don't you two round up some others and keep watch over the fence in case the attackers come back. Better be safe than sorry. I'll head back to the lake and keep the other QRF teams on alert in case we get hit again from some other direction."

At first light, they began recovering the bodies of the 11 residents killed: six men, two women, and three children. A total of 15 other residents were wounded and had been helped or carried to Julia's aid station. Three entire families had been wiped out, killed or captured, as well as several of the QRF team members, guards, and nearby homeowners who had joined the fight.

In all, 14 residents were dead or captured, and two of the 15 wounded would later die at the aid station soon after they arrived. Julia had to triage the large number of wounded, and the two men were beyond hope of saving. She had to make some hard choices in order to save those she had the ability and supplies to save, and let the two go that she could not. There were tears in her eyes as she worked on the others, but Bill and his kids, Wayne and Nichole, understood her decision. That didn't make it easier on any of them though.

After the bodies of the residents had been recovered, six bodies of the attackers had been dragged into the streets from the back and side yards of the houses that were attacked. One of the bodies had a plank of wood stuck on his chest. Obviously, someone had remembered the advice about booby-trapping the back door with a trip wire and a board with long nails driven into it. One or more of the nails must have pierced the man's heart.

There were four more attackers who had been wounded badly enough that they couldn't escape over the fence. One of them was a woman. Another bled out and died leaning against the back fence.

Undoubtedly there were several others among the attacking force who had been wounded, but managed to climb back over the fence and escape, as no one pursued them, except for Donna and Ed, and the rooftop guard, firing at them as they retreated into the woods. Later in the morning seven more bodies were found between the fence and the wood lines on either side. The total dead among the attackers was 13, plus the three prisoners. The numbers of casualties on both sides was probably pretty even- except the Sea Breezes fighters had repelled the attack. They had won. Or more accurately, they had survived.

Josh examined the three prisoners and decided it was OK to move them, although one of them would need assistance. He called Richard over and pointed to the back of the man who was able to stand. He wore a leather jacket with "Werewolves" stenciled on the back.

Richard just shook his head and said, "Sonofabitch."

# Chapter 45

As the wounded homeowners began arriving at the aid station, the less serious wounded were transferred over to Bill Thornton's place to make room for the more critical patients in Julia's house, where they had lights and where most of the supplies were. Bill had a couple of guys fire up the generator and hook up some lights in each room of Julia's house. Volunteers from the community came over to help care for the wounded.

By dawn, of the 15 wounded, counting the two who had died overnight, 10 were still in Julia's and Bill's homes on beds or pallets. Five homeowners with non-life-threatening wounds had been treated and sent back to their homes, with orders to get some rest and return later in the afternoon for a more complete checkup.

Richard had returned from the lake at first light, and he and Josh, with the help of two other homeowners, had taken the three captives to the picnic area, tied their legs and arms behind their backs, blindfolded them, put duct tape over their mouths, then chained each of them to one of the BBQ stands.

One of the QRF men who was not involved in the fight was designated to guard them. He was instructed to remain alert and to stay at least five yards away from the prisoners until Richard came to get them later in the morning.

Richard told the prisoners, "Your wounds are not going to be treated until we have treated our wounded. You will not be allowed to relieve yourselves, drink, or talk. Any attempt to escape will mean you will be immediately shot." He looked over at the guard to make sure he had heard, and the guard nodded, indicating he understood the instructions.

Richard and Josh went back to check on the guard situation and make sure that all the rooftop guard posts had been relieved, and that the new guards were alert. They put the word out that the morning meeting would be postponed until 1 p.m. so that the residents could take time to recover, and maybe get a little rest. Then they went back to their homes to check on their families and get a few hours before dealing with the prisoners, figuring the time gagged, tied up, and chained would soften them up and make them more willing to talk. They agreed to meet at the picnic area at 11 o'clock.

Not many of the homeowners had gotten any sleep after all the noise and commotion created by the attackers and the deploying QRF's. After getting such a shock, many decided that rather than sleeping they would use the time to further barricade their homes; others went over to help out at the aid station.

## Chapter 46

A few minutes before 11 a.m., Josh got up and put the word out through his security forces leaders for all the QRF members, and all the guards except those on duty, to meet at 12:30 p.m. at the playground area. After getting that done, he walked over to the picnic area and joined Richard.

While Richard and the guard kept their guns ready, Josh unlocked each prisoner one at a time and took them across the street to relieve themselves in a neighbor's refuse pit. One of the men had been shot in the leg, and Josh had to virtually carry him over while Richard came along with his gun pointed at the man. After each had relieved themselves, Josh gave the prisoner a drink of water from a tin can, tied them up, and locked them back in their previous positions.

Julia arrived a little later, with some bandages and antiseptics and even though she was exhausted, did the best she could to patch up their wounds; one man had a deep furrow cut into his scalp by a bullet, and the woman had been shot in the shoulder. The most serious wound was the leg wound, as the bullet had also broken the shinbone. Julia then went back to her home for some much-needed sleep. She told Richard she would be at the 1 p.m. meeting to give an update on the wounded.

Josh stood guard as Richard took each prisoner one at a time out to the street to interrogate them. He started with the woman.

"What's your name?"

"Maria Hernandez. Can I have some more water?"

"After you answer my questions. First, where did you all park your bikes and cars?"

"Listen, I'll answer all of your questions. I just joined the Werewolves because my boyfriend has been buggin' me to. The son of a bitch left me wounded in a back yard, and ran away and jumped the fence, so I don't owe those assholes anything.

"Anyway, we parked them about a half mile from the east and west sides of the entrance to Sea Breezes, along Connor Drive. They left one guy to guard each location, and I think they left four or five to guard our new home base. The rest of us came though the woods on each side and attacked you from the north corners."

"Where are the Werewolves camped out?"

"We moved into what's left of Pelican's Landing. We had a run-in with the Zulus at first, but we made a pact with them and we don't mess with each other. They told us about what happened when they hit you guys here in Sea Breezes, about the rooftop guards, but our fuckin' know-it-all leader thought he was smarter and could make a plan that would capture part of Sea Breezes so we could sack it. No one told us about those extra forces that showed up- we thought we just had to deal with the guards and the homeowners."

"Yeah, well we'll be even better prepared next time."

"What are you going to do with me?"

"I don't know yet. I'm not through asking you questions, so it depends on how cooperative you are."

"I'll tell you everything I know, mister, I just want to go back home and shoot that cowardly asshole boyfriend of mine."

Richard nodded and said, "How many of there are you? I mean total gang members and women and children."

"I'm not sure of the exact number, but I think there were about 40 or 50 of us, but only eight or ten women and a few kids. Part of their plan was to grab some women here too."

"Yeah, they got away with two women and one teenage girl. Who are those other two men over there?"

"One is named Jake something and the other guy, the one who was shot in the leg, calls himself 'Stalin'. I don't know what his real name is, but he's, like, the number two man behind the leader, John King. Everyone just calls him 'King" because he likes that. King and Stalin, ha! They're both a couple o' macho assholes, but they're pretty hard guys."

"OK, I appreciate your cooperation, and if it turns out you're telling me the truth, I'll take that into account in deciding what to do with you. But it also depends on whether or not your buddies over there tell the same story. Get up, I'm taking you back."

The next two men weren't as forthcoming as Maria was. But they knew Maria must have been talking so they more or less corroborated her information. Richard tied them back up the way they were, and walked down to Josh's house.

A relief guard came over for the man who had guarded the prisoners all morning, and after he arrived, Josh and Richard went over to the playground area to talk to the guards and QRF members.

# Chapter 47

Sean Koenig and Wayne Thornton were only a few months apart in age, and since they were in the same grade at school, they had become friends. Wayne had even gone shooting with Sean and his dad once in awhile, and he was a pretty good shot.

While his mom and sister were busy in the house and his dad was getting some much-needed rest after the horrific attack of the previous night, Sean walked over to the Thornton's house, and after watching Wayne empty a bedpan in the front yard waste pit, took his friend aside and sat under the live oak tree in front of his house.

"Wayne, my dad is going to reorganize the guard and QRF teams this morning. What do you think about you and me joining them? You'll be 15 this month, and I know you can shoot. I think you can do more good as a guard than emptying bedpans, and besides, Anita said she wanted to help out Nichole in the aid station. I bet if you talked to your dad and Julia, and told them that Anita would take your place, maybe we could convince our dads to let us on the guard force. I've already talked to Anita, and she wants to help out over here anyway."

"Sean, I'd been thinking that same thing as I was patching up the wounded men and women from the security forces this morning. They are going to need replacements, and I'd rather be doing something to help out with our security. I'll ask my dad and see if it's OK with him."

"Good. If it's all right with your dad, just come to the 12:30 meeting of the security forces at the playground. If you don't show up, I'll know he said no."

Later, at the playground, Sean had a big grin on his face when he saw Wayne jogging towards the group of security men and women as they were assembling. Wayne just nodded his head and smiled back.

Josh hollered out, "Listen up, folks. We need to reconstitute the guard and QRF teams, and we need more people. I've added my son, Sean, to the guard force and I see Wayne Thornton's dad has given permission to his son to be on the security forces also. He'll be on a QRF team."

"So, we're down to using 15 year-olds in the security force. I've made out two lists, one for the guard force and another for the four QRF teams. But we've got some holes to fill in the QRF teams even with adding Wayne, so you all need to talk to your neighbors and family members to see if they would join up. We need three more people to serve in the QRF's. We no longer have a restriction on single parents, if one of their kids is at least 15 years old, and we'll take any other male or female age 15 or older, as long as they know how to handle weapons and have had shooting experience.

"Once we fill up each QRF team with five people, the commanders can take them out back to the Phase II area and drill them again. Obviously last night was a close call, and if the Werewolves had a larger force or were better planners, Sea Breezes could have lost a lot more people. There are still desperate and unscrupulous thugs out there and probably some other gangs. If the Zulus and the Werewolves were to link up, we would be hard pressed to stop them unless our QRF teams are filled, trained and, by the way, react quicker."

One of the QRF team members raised his hand and said, "Josh, I know we have to get better and react quicker, but I was one of the three in the second QRF that showed up, and the reason the fourth, our commander, didn't show was because he was in one of the houses that were captured, and he was killed defending his family."

Another homeowner spoke up and said, "Yeah, but I went to Gary Holmes' house after it was all over to see why he hadn't joined our team at the rallying point. He told me he wasn't going to be part of anything except protecting his own house. He did train with us, but he was a no-show last night."

Silence descended and Josh fumed. "I'll talk to Richard about that and we'll deal with him. But we still need to come up with a better plan. From now on, if there is any shooting, we can't just have a primary and a standby QRF team any more. Any shooting means all four QRF's assemble and the primary team on duty moves immediately to the fighting. We'll rotate each week to have the other three teams assemble at the picnic area to act as a reserve for the first team deployed, or in case the first attack is a feint, and another attack comes somewhere else along our perimeter.

"Anything else? OK, you all might as well stick around here for the one o'clock meeting. I'll go talk to Richard about Holmes. And, you commanders- once we fill your team, drill them more, and practice quickly assembling at your rallying points."

# Chapter 48

As the homeowners moved towards the usual meeting place at the picnic area, Richard and Josh steered them over to the playground area, away from the prisoners and their guard. Once everyone had gathered, Richard stood with his back to the fence and gave them a brief run down of what had happened the night before. Josh went over his meeting with the security forces about reconstituting the QRF teams, mentioning particularly the new age and status rules for inclusion, and that he still had three holes to fill. He asked for any new volunteers to see him after the meeting.

Julia gave a brief summary of the casualties, mentioning that in addition to the two who had died shortly after arriving at the aid station, one more had died late that morning. "I just don't have enough supplies. I need sheets or something I can use as bandages, thread I can use for stitching, and any type of antiseptics or antibiotics you have: rubbing alcohol, antiseptic creams, hydrogen peroxide, soap, and even Clorox. We're out of antibiotic tablets. Richard, can we make another run to the hospital and pharmacies? People are dying that could be saved if I had the medical supplies I need."

Richard said he would organize another scavenger hunt, but not until tomorrow. He said he would discuss that tomorrow at the 9 a.m. meeting after he gave it some thought. "But today we have other problems to deal with."

"First, just so you know, Josh and I have been talking about coming up with some way to get our three women back. A raid is out of the question though. Josh will be talking to some of the QRF teams for ideas, but I think we're going to try for a prisoner exchange with the Werewolves- their three for our three women. Josh and I have worked out a preliminary plan, and I won't bore you with the details, but we're going to give it a try if we can get enough support.

"Second, seeing as how Gary Holmes didn't show up for this meeting, I've gotten four men from the guard force and as soon as we finish up here, we're going to go over to his house and arrest him for deliberately not showing up at his QRF rallying point last night. He blew off his duty and he told one of his team members this morning that he wasn't going to be participating in the QRF anymore. I've also talked to Donna Fleer and she's going to get three jurors and we're going to have a trial tomorrow afternoon and see what they decide to do with Holmes.

"Right now, go back to your homes and if you haven't already, reinforce your barricades. I'll see you at the meeting tomorrow morning."

# Chapter 49

After the meeting, Richard met with the three men and one woman who would accompany him to Gary Holmes' house to make the arrest. "I need for two of you to go around to the back of his house from one house over so he doesn't see you. You two guys come with me to the front door and cover me. I'm going to knock on the door, and if he doesn't open, I'll kick or shoot it open. If he shoots at us, shoot to kill him. Once we have him in custody, we'll tie him up and take him over to the picnic area and chain him to one of the BBQ grill posts. Any questions?"

There were none, so they set out for Holmes' house. Two houses before Holmes', one man and one woman turned off to get through the back yards to the rear of Holmes' house. Richard gave them three minutes, then he and the other two men walked up to the front door.

With one man pointing a rifle and the other a shotgun on either side of him, Richard drew his Bersa and knocked on the door. He knocked again and much to his surprise, Holmes opened the front door. He had a pistol in his hand, but didn't point it at Richard. He had apparently been looking out his back door window and had seen the armed man move into his back yard, and figured out what was going on.

"I'm not going to fight since I'm outnumbered, but you got no right to come here with armed men. I didn't do anything."

"Well, Gary, that's the point. You were supposed to show up and help fight off the attackers last night and you just blew everything and everyone off and let a lot of good men and women do the fighting for you. As a result, more of them were probably killed or wounded than should have been. Maybe a couple of them wouldn't have been shot if you had been there shooting too. I warned everyone that they had to pitch in on defending our community or there would be consequences. You're under arrest, and we're going to put you on trial for desertion under enemy fire. Drop your gun and put you arms behind your back."

Holmes was essentially a coward, and did as he was told. Richard tied his hands behind his back and the arresting force led him over to the picnic area, chained him to the last BBQ post, then tied his feet together. The guard who had been guarding the three Werewolves now guarded Holmes also. The guard told Holmes to keep his mouth shut or he would be gagged like the other prisoners.

While this was going on, Josh had driven his car over to the picnic area, and Jacob Hanson and Leroy Ivory followed with their pickup trucks. They also had with them one of the five-man QRF teams. All of the men and women on the QRF had volunteered for the exchange mission, but Josh didn't want to appear like an attacking force by taking everyone, so he decided it would be best to take one complete team that was already used to working together.

They unlocked Maria, and she was put in the back of the lead pickup. They tied her hands behind her back and pulled a hood over her head. She had protested, but they told her they didn't want her to see any more of the inside of their community than she already had. All three vehicles had a stick with a white flag made of pillowcases attached, and guns pointing outward in case of trouble. The three vehicles drove off towards Pelican's Landing.

When they were a few blocks away from the gated entrance, they stopped and took off Maria's hood, and stood her up in the back of Leroy's pickup As Leroy was doing that, everyone but the vehicles' drivers dismounted and spread out. The QRF team and Josh got out and split up as they had planned, taking one white flag on either side of Leroy's slowly advancing truck with a white flag flying from its aerial. When they got about 50 yards from the gate, Josh walked up with his white flag and said, "Ahoy there, Werewolves! My name is Josh, from Sea Breezes. We came to talk. We have Maria, as you can see, and we also have Stalin and Jake back in Sea Breezes. We need to talk to King about you getting all three of them back."

The guards saw the deployed forces from Sea Breezes, and seeing the white flags, didn't fire on them. One of the guards on the gate spoke to another guard, who then trotted off towards the houses. The man who was apparently in charge of the guards hollered, "You all stay where you are. Don't come any closer, and keep your weapons pointed down. There are rifles on you, and if anyone comes any closer, we'll kill you first, Josh."

After a long 15-minute wait, a big man came up to the gate, opened it, and said, "I'm King. What the hell do you fuckers want?"

Maria, answered, "King! Stalin and Jake are wounded, but they're alive. I got hit in the shoulder. They want to do an exchange- us for the three women you took."

King looked surprised and said, "Are you sure Stalin is OK?"

"Yeah, he took a bullet in the leg, but he'll live. Jake just had a bullet crease his head that knocked him out. These guys had some nurse patch us up and she splint Stalin's leg, but we all need some medical attention from that Indian doctor you captured."

Josh spoke up and said, "If you agree, we'll meet you on neutral ground, at the McDonald's where Beach Parkway meets Sea Breezes Drive, at four this afternoon. We'll stop and have your three Werewolves on our side of McDonald's and you guys can stop on Beach Parkway with our women. We'll meet in the middle with one pickup from each side, and swap prisoners. No more than the driver and one man with each pickup's prisoners."

King thought about this for a few moments and called the guard in charge over for a brief discussion. In the prolonged silence, Maria yelled out, "King, please do this. They'll kill us if you don't, and Stalin needs to get help quick."

King finally said, "OK, we'll be there at four, but we're coming in force, and if you fuck with us, we'll waste you." He then turned around and walked away.

Josh pulled everyone back, got Maria down from Leroy's pickup, slid the hood back over Maria's head, and put her in the front seat of the car. Josh turned his car around and the pickups followed as they headed back towards Sea Breezes.

On the way back, instead of following Josh, Jacob and Leroy pulled their vehicles, with the five-man QRF, off Beach Parkway on a street just before Sea Breezes Drive. They entered the Home Depot parking lot, and with an extension ladder set up in the back of Leroy's pickup, climbed up onto the roof of the Home Depot building. From there they looked out about 30 yards away onto Beach Parkway from behind the concrete ledge of the Home Depot roof.

The QRF team members were all armed with AR-15 rifles and they had dozens of loaded 30-round magazines. Former Gunnery Sergeant Leroy Ivory split the QRF team up along the roof's ledge between the two corners facing Beach Parkway, and after checking out their firing positions, their weapons, and their ammo, he showed each shooter where his or her firing position would be, and let them sight in their weapons on various objects to get a feel for where targets might appear in each of their assigned fields of fire.

"Listen up everybody. Wait for me to fire first. I'll shoot at whichever vehicle, probably a motorcycle, is in the lead and that will be your signal to open up. Karinne, you concentrate your fire on the first car or truck. Ed, you shoot at whichever car or truck is next. One or both of the Werewolves' leaders, King and Stalin, will probably be in one of those since Stalin was wounded and King will probably be debriefing him on the way home. The rest of you fire at other cars or bikes, and don't stop firing except to change magazines. Keep firing as long as there is anyone who shows any sign of movement."

He looked over at Malcolm, Kathryn Brown's 16-year old son and said, "Malcolm, are you OK with this?"

"Yes sir. They attacked us and killed our neighbors, and I was friends with one of the girls they captured. I don't have any problem with shooting the bastards who did that."

"Good man. Anyone have any questions? OK, let's settle down, and remember to stay below the roof's ledge and out of sight. I'll let you know when I hear from Josh if we're a go or not."

After each man and woman knew what to do on his signal, Leroy told them to go to their positions, lie down, and get some rest. He then lay down with the radio by his head and closed his eyes.

Meanwhile, Josh continued on to the Sea Breezes entrance. When he arrived in front of his house, he stopped, left his car running, and got out of the car. After a few seconds, he yelled out to no one, "Guys, I'll take her from here. Wait here for me and we'll talk about how we're going to deploy at McDonald's."

He got back into his car, revved the engine and said to Maria, "I'm going to take you back to the picnic area now and tie you up again. As you'll see, we've arrested a guy from our community and he's tied up there also. Don't say anything to anyone."

On arriving at the picnic area, Josh took her out of the car, removed her hood, taped her mouth shut, and chained her back in the usual manner. He then told the three Werewolves, "We've arranged a swap for you this afternoon. Keep your mouths shut and behave, or the guard will shoot you. If you behave and don't cause any trouble for us, you'll be back in Pelican's Landing in a few hours."

Josh walked away with a grim smile on his face.

# Chapter 50

At 3:45 p.m., Josh led a four-vehicle convoy out of Sea Breezes in a neighbor's big pickup, with the three Werewolves in the bed, along with two guards. Spread out among the other three vehicles and their drivers were two of the QRF teams. The one remaining QRF team, other than the one with Leroy, was left behind, assembled at the picnic area, to defend the neighborhood in case the Werewolves used the exchange as a ruse to attack Sea Breezes, or in case of any other trouble. The prisoners were blindfolded before they left. On arrival at the McDonald's, the two QRF teams unloaded and spread out on each side of Sea Breezes Drive.

At a little after four p.m. Josh saw the Werewolves convoy, consisting of a pickup, two cars, and about a dozen motorcycles, pull up and stop on Beach Parkway. All the men got out with their rifles unslung, but pointed down at the ground, just like the QRF team members had done. As they had agreed, Josh, with Richard riding shotgun, drove the pickup halfway towards the Werewolves, and they did the same with their pickup. Richard and Josh took the blindfolds off the prisoners, untied their hands, and had them get out of the pickup's bed and stand off to the side. Josh helped "Stalin" get down and walk over to the other two.

The two women and the girl climbed out of the Werewolves' pickup on shaky legs, bloodied and tearful. Josh grimaced at the sight, but he and Richard transferred the wounded prisoners to the Werewolves' pickup as the women staggered over to Josh's.

With wary caution, the two pickups returned with their former prisoners to their own people. After brief exchanges with the sobbing women, it was clear to Josh that they had been raped and beaten. Just after the Werewolves drove off, Josh picked up his walkie-talkie, keyed the mike, and said. "Gunny, we were right. Execute."

Leroy Ivory frowned in disgust and replied, "Roger, out."

He gave the high sign to his force, which counting himself and another driver, consisted of a total of seven men and women. They all moved to their positions, raised their rifles up over the ledge, and keeping a low profile, sighted on Beach Parkway, and waited.

When the lead motorcycle appeared, Leroy tracked him and held his fire until he had reached the end of their position, but was still in range. He then initiated the ambush with a well-aimed shot that brought the lead rider down. Then all seven AR's opened up on the convoy that followed.

It was a bloodbath. The cars and the pickup were stopped, riddled with bullets. Only two motorcycles managed to escape the barrage and the riders, seeing their comrades fall all around them, accelerated out of range as fast as they could. None of the Werewolves even got a shot off in the confusion and hail of bullets.

The rest of the gang members were killed, including King and Stalin. Effectively, the Werewolves were no longer a force to contend with. The few remaining gang members would have a hard enough time just defending their Pelican's Landing turf.

Unfortunately, Maria was also killed in the onslaught of bullets, but she never should have participated in the attack in the first place, and she paid the price. Leroy was not supposed to initiate the ambush unless he heard from Josh about the condition of the women. There was no doubt that they had been beaten and raped, and that was the purpose of the ambush- revenge, and removing scum from the earth, on the prearranged code word, "Execute."

# Chapter 51

At the 9 a.m. meeting, Richard and Josh gave a summary of the arrest, and the prisoner exchange and ambush. Richard noted that it was the first time that the Sea Breezes community had gone on the offensive, and because of good planning and execution, they had taken no casualties, thanks in large part to Leroy Ivory's planning and the QRF team's marksmanship.

After Richard had finished his briefing, Donna Fleer stood up and gave her news. "This morning I was tuning in my radio on Ham radio frequencies like I've been doing every morning, and I picked up another message from the President. I listened to the transmission twice, and took notes. I'll read them to you all, but like the last time, this isn't an exact transcript."

"The President apologized for the delay in communications, but said that security considerations prohibited any update of the first message until now.

"The President's family and the White House staff were rescued by a joint task force of the Armed Forces. They were flown away in full nuclear decontamination suits by helicopter to an unnamed secure location where the staffs of all major government organizations are being reconstituted from the survivors of the various agencies and departments.

"The captured terrorists were interrogated and eventually gave up names, leading to the capture of an Iranian illegal in New Jersey, whose name sounded like Sa-yeed Ma-mudy or something like that- his name wasn't spelled out. He was also interrogated, I assume using "enhanced" techniques, and admitted that Iran was behind the attacks, in coordination with several Islamic terrorist groups. He also said that he was told that China and Russia had assisted in initiating cyber attacks that almost completely shut down the United States. This was later verified by the CIA and the FBI.

"Navy submarines and Air Force bombers have leveled the remaining infrastructure of Iran, and the U.S. initiated a series of devastating cyber attacks against them, as well as the Chinese and Russians. There were no physical attacks against China or Russia, but their infrastructure and communications have been brought down, just like ours was, only worse. Due to the lack of preparation by their citizens, the effects are even more severe than what we suffered. The Chinese and Russians were warned that any further attacks of any kind against the United States would elicit a nuclear response, and so far, there has been no retaliation from either nation. After the U.S.'s leveling of Iran, they appear to be taking the threat seriously.

"Europe is recovering more slowly, and their recovery is proceeding unevenly. England and Germany are about where we are, but many of the other European countries hit, like France, Spain, and Italy are still struggling. Israel suffered many attacks from neighboring terrorist groups, and although they suffered a lot of casualties, no Mideast nation initiated any large-scale attacks, fearing Israel's nuclear retaliation.

"Many of the National Guard and the Reserve units have been reconstituted and are operational, along with most of the stateside military units. Some of the U.S. forces from overseas have returned to join our U.S.-based forces, and are switching from defensive postures to concentrating on the problems of the seven cities and two Army posts that suffered nuclear contamination, along with the huge problem of refugees that fled those and other cities and military bases.

"Although the entire structure of the world's economies has been disrupted, our allies and friends around the world are sending assistance, especially Japan, Canada and Australia, who were not targeted. Areas around many of our port cities and some major airports are slowly recovering, since food and medical supplies are being delivered from other countries. Local communications, electricity, and water have been restored in many of these areas.

"At some later date, food, medical supplies, and some fuel will begin to be trucked in or air dropped to designated regional locations in the U.S. for distribution by National Guard and other military units, in coordination with local government authorities. The National Emergency Alert System is expected to be functional nationwide in the next few weeks, and in the larger metropolitan areas some local radio and even TV stations are functioning.

"All of this will take awhile, maybe several months in some areas. For now, the President urged all Americans to avoid violence, cooperate with one another, and hang tough."

Donna's reading was interrupted in many areas with cheers and shouts, as relief spread across many faces. Among those who also understood the negative part of Donna's report was Richard.

"Neighbors, we have reason to celebrate, but remember that realistically we may have to continue on our own for several months. Celebrate, but remember our current situation hasn't changed. We still need to be security-minded, and work on alternate food sources.

"And speaking of food, we will be sending out hunting and fishing parties tomorrow morning, and we will also organize another scavenging trip, concentrating on medical supplies and any types of food we can scrounge. With the decimation of the Werewolves, the remnants of which are probably consolidating and fortifying their positions to protect themselves from the Zulus, our security situation has improved enough for another outing, but not enough to drop our guard in any way."

# Chapter 52

At 1 p.m., Donna Fleer and three jurors set up Gary Holmes' living room for a trial. Richard and several others did a thorough search of his home and found a small hoard of food of various types in the walk-in closet of the second bedroom. Some of this may have been stolen from other homes during the two attacks, or while neighbors were out on guard duty, as a lot more than his share of the salvaged food from the churches was found. The food was left in place to be distributed later, along with the proceeds from the next day's hunting and fishing outings. They also found several weapons and hundreds of rounds of ammunition, which they carried over to Josh's house for use by the security forces.

The trial began with Donna reading the charges, which included the most serious one of desertion, but also including theft of food from other houses, and the attempted theft of Jacob Hanson's dried food. Holmes was represented by Fred Carlucci, who argued that "Judge" Donna didn't have the authority to conduct a trial or impose any sentences, an interesting about face for someone who had tried to get elected to that position. Donna, as a prosecuting Judge, counter-argued that she was elected by the only authority still in existence in their area, the people of the Sea Breezes community, and the trial went forward

Testimony was received from members of Holmes' QRF team concerning his desertion of the force, and his confession that he wasn't going to participate in QRF deployments. Evidence of the existence of his large hoard of presumably stolen food was presented, and testimony from Jacob and witnesses to the theft attempt at the bazaar was heard. Holmes refused to testify on his behalf, merely saying he didn't recognize any authority over over him by this "kangaroo court."

It didn't take long for the verdicts to come in from the jury: guilty on desertion; not guilty of food theft (as there was not enough direct evidence that definitely proved that the items of food that he had had been stolen); guilty of attempted theft of the dried fruit. Donna sentenced him to expulsion from the community.

He would be allowed to depart with a backpack full of food and clothing and whatever other items from his home that he wanted to carry with him. He would be driven to the edge of the bridge and given one weapon and some ammunition and be left there. He was warned that if he attempted to return, he would be shot on sight by the guards or other homeowners.

Holmes fumed during the reading of the sentence and at the end made a lunge for Donna and grabbed her by the throat. Richard reacted quickly, pulled his Bersa, and slammed the barrel down hard on Holmes' head. He grunted, went limp and rolled off Donna, bleeding and unable to move. They tied him up, and when he regained consciousness, led him back to the picnic area and chained him to the BBQ post again.

## Chapter 53

At the 9 a.m. meeting, the neighbors were notified of the jury's verdict of the Holmes trial, as well as his sentence. Josh had unshackled him that morning and allowed him back in his home, under guard, to fill a backpack with food and other items he wanted to take. Josh led him out of his house in front of a crowd of his neighbors as Leroy Ivory drove up in his pickup truck. Holmes was loaded in the bed and tied down, and his backpack was thrown in beside him.

Josh climbed in the back with Holmes, along with two members of the guard force for added security. They drove Holmes out of Sea Breezes and to the Phelps Island side of the bridge to Port Monroe. One of the guards walked out on the bridge about 100 yards, and set an unloaded semi-auto pistol with two empty magazines and a box of ammunition down on the road.

The two former Gunnery Sergeants, pulled Holmes out of the pickup's bed, untied him, and handed him his backpack. Josh glared at him and said, "Holmes, there is nothing I hate more than a coward who will abandon his friends during battle. You should have been shot for desertion, but because of the judge's sentence, you get a chance to live. If I were you I'd take my chances in Port Monroe. Phelps Island is now controlled by the Zulus and us, and I don't think you will fare well with the Zulus. And I promise you, if I ever see you again, I will kill you." With that, Josh got back into the pickup and Leroy drove off and left Holmes standing at the bridge.

The homeowners watched Leroy's pickup pull out of the Sea Breezes entrance. Once they were out of sight, Richard addressed the crowd. "Folks, we had another successful hunt this morning, including one deer and a few wild dogs and cats. Another 33 fish were caught in our lake. In addition, a fishing team went out through the forest and marsh to the ocean and from what they told me, managed to land a couple of dozen fish, and a medium size shark, which scared the hell out of them." Richard smiled and everyone chuckled at the thought of the surprise of the angler as he landed his catch.

"The hunters and fishermen are now butchering, cleaning, and smoking the fish and meat they brought back. At 5 o'clock this afternoon, come to the former Holmes house and we'll do our normal distribution, including some food that Holmes had stolen and hoarded. Sophia will meet again with the truly needy families after this meeting and make sure they are taken care of.

"At 1 p.m. anyone who wants to go out on a scavenging hunt, please meet at the lake. I know that some of your have cars that are out, or almost out, of gas, so if you can't drive, siphon off whatever gas is in the bottom of your tanks and bring it with you.

"Last night Josh and I made a plan and mapped out the scavenging route we'll be taking, and it will include the hospital and all stand-alone pharmacies and grocery stores, some more restaurants and school cafeterias, and other places that many wouldn't think of searching. We may not get much food, but I expect we'll be able to get some medical supplies for Julia's aid station. We will make sure that the guards are on duty and we'll leave two QRF teams behind in case of an attack.

"By the way, the Holmes house has been designated our new Community Center. It will serve as a meeting area for the security forces, as a food distribution point, and a storage location for any items we are able to scrounge going forward, It will also be our courtroom, in the unlikely event we have another trial.

"I guess that's about it. If there are no questions, I'll see some of you here at 1, and the rest of you at the Community Center at 5."

With that, the gathered neighbors dispersed to head back home, and Richard went over and waited for Sophia to finish talking with the heads of the needy families. He thought to himself, "All of this is getting to be pretty routine."

# EPILOGUE

June 3, 2018

It was Sean Koenig who first saw the helicopter, a Florida National Guard Blackhawk, flying over the Port Monroe oil refinery and downtown area from his rooftop guard position. He was so excited he fired off three rounds from his rifle out towards the ocean. This of course brought a reaction from the QRF team on duty as well as alarming the whole neighborhood, which in hindsight, was as good a way as any to get the word out. Certainly no one was angry with the young man for alerting everyone to the good news.

In the United States, the president had continued the periodic updates, and the FEMA national emergency radio system had been restored in the first week in March. Even so, the president had used both the FEMA radio system and the Ham radio network to send out his communications, since most citizens were used to getting the messages on their battery-powered Ham radios, and the power was still out over the majority of the country. Although the messages always had an encouraging outlook, reading between the lines it was obvious that the government was still struggling with the problem of trying to settle the millions who had fled the dirty bomb target areas, as well as the millions who had fled all the other large cities and military bases fearing such an attack.

The situation had been relatively peaceful and uneventful in Sea Breezes over the last three months. There were no major security events, except for two night attacks by small groups- apparently unsuspecting elements from Port Monroe, who were unaware of Sea Breezes' defenses. The attacks were quickly repelled by the roof guards, assisted by quick reacting homeowners in the areas hit. By the time the QRF teams on duty had arrived, the attackers had already been driven off, and there were no casualties among the Sea Breezes' fighters.

A sort of non-aggression pact had been made with the Zulu Warriors when Richard had led a contingent of two QRF teams, similar to what they had done with the Werewolves, out to Sunset Beach Estates for a talk. After an initial verbal standoff, Richard had met with the gang's leader at the gated entrance. After a brief discussion they agreed it was in both of their interests to leave each other alone, since they all knew that the government was in the initial phases of reconstituting, and help would be arriving to Port Monroe soon.

Richard reminded the gang leader that the military or police authorities would take a dim view of the Zulus having killed scores of people and stolen their houses, and that they might want to think about moving back to Port Monroe to their own turf soon. They hadn't yet, but Richard knew they wouldn't be in Sunset Beach when the Army or police forces arrived, especially now that the first Army helicopter had been seen over the city.

By the beginning of June, the situation in Sea Breezes had stabilized, as the community adjusted to the new normal of their harsh existence. More frequent scavenging trips, that included every possible source of food and supplies, including abandoned homes as well as small stores of all types, had yielded not only some food, but also some medical supplies. The improved security situation allowed them to take more time to thoroughly search all areas in detail. Locked storage rooms and cabinets in the upper floors of the hospital, and in the island's CVS and Walgreens stand alone pharmacies, yielded some more antibiotics, prescription drugs, and over the counter medicine and other medical supplies. Julia was very pleased, and her aid station was able to handle most of the community's medical problems.

Sea Breezes had sustained a few more deaths: two more men had died of complications from previous gunshot wounds sustained during the Werewolves' attack; one woman had died in childbirth from loss of blood; and there had been one heart attack and one suicide. But otherwise her patient load was down, and consisted mostly of non-life-threatening illnesses and diseases, such as flu, diarrhea, infections, skin rashes, and sprains.

Canned and packaged food had been found in a few of the stores, homes, and restaurants they had searched, and the first vegetables from home gardens were being harvested. There were even some oranges and grapefruit popping up at the bazaars from back yard trees neighbors had planted when they first moved into the Sea Breezes. Richard and Sophia had delighted over their first tomato and first orange in three months, and they had gotten used to eating a lot of fish. They, like everyone else, had lost considerable weight, and some of their less prepared neighbors were downright skinny.

Fish had become more plentiful because the fishermen had been able to branch out to other areas, accompanied by their security forces, and now went out daily and stayed out fishing longer. The hunters still brought in some varied types of meat, but the supply of edible animals was almost exhausted on the small island. Fortunately, with winter ending in Canada, flocks of geese often rested from their journey northward in their lake, and were harvested. The lake's duck population had long since been depleted.

The Koenigs and the Cantrells had only a few items left of packaged food- actually just a few large containers of freeze dried meals and a few MREs. Both families had given away some of their supplies to the families in need who had children to feed.

After the second sighting of helicopters, this time of several scout helicopters over both the city and the Port Monroe airport, the old friends met at the Koenig's house to celebrate, and after a meager dinner, the four adults sat down with the last of their Jack Daniels and Cokes. Their shared evening meal had consisted of some fish, a freeze-dried mix of berries, MRE crackers, and two small tomatoes.

Anita and Sean were in the front yard playing with Natasha, who wasn't quite as lively as she was before her wound. She was still fairly young she healed quickly, although not completely. Like Richard, she would always have a bit of a limp. But she was again able to enjoy being chased, and fetching tennis balls for the kids. Natasha had also lost a lot of weight, but after saving Richard's life, there was no way that he was not going to feed her regularly. Not all of the families in the neighborhood did that for their pets.

Sophia took her first sip in months of their favorite cocktail, smiled and sighed. "I'm glad we saved a little for this occasion. This is really special. I'm getting really tired of drinking only water with a Clorox taste. Who knows when we'll get a chance to have cocktails again?"

Carmen smiled and said, "Yeah, I guess it will be awhile, but what I miss the most is being able to take a long, hot shower. Bathing out of a bucket is not my idea of clean. I think that is what I'm most looking forward to in the future. It's funny how the little things we've always taken for granted are what we miss the most."

Richard said, "Well it goes without saying that we all miss having a steady supply of all kinds of food whenever we wanted it. Just think about how great it would be now to be able to drive down and get a Big Mac for supper; or for that matter, to have enough gas in our cars make the trip."

There was a contemplative silence over these thoughts, until the quiet was broken by Josh. "Rich, did you ever think we'd be fighting battles again? Man, I retired to get away from being shot at, but as soon as I got to my retirement home, I had to go to war again."

Richard looked at his old friend and said, "Yeah, but I think we did pretty good, helping to organize a group of civilians to defend themselves. Many of the men and women worked as hard as we did, and some were truly heroic; I'm thinking of people like Donna, Bill, Jacob and Julia. And, let's face it, it took a lot of dedication and bravery to be a rooftop guard. Everyone was at the very least cooperative- even Fred, once he realized that we were on our own. It just goes to show you that Americans can still rise to the occasion and take up arms to defend themselves and their communities when they have to."

"Yeah, and I won't forget the other veterans, especially Leroy Ivory- that man made me proud to be a Marine. All of the vets pitched in with help and encouragement wherever they could. But, man, I'm just glad it's coming to an end soon. We still have a ways to go though. It ain't over 'til it's over."

At the end of the evening, as the sun was setting over the horizon of the Sea Breezes homes, Sophia and Richard, with Natasha at their side, strolled back to their house, hand in hand. When they got home, Richard and Sophia undressed, gave each other a long kiss, and went to bed, snuggling in each other's arms.

The next morning, after Sophia and Richard had finished their small breakfast and fed Natasha, they heard a loud and unfamiliar sound above them. They ran out into the front yard to see what the racket was. They saw an amazing sight- three Air Force C-130 cargo planes had passed over Phelps Island and were descending slowly on short final approach to the Port Monroe airport.

Richard and Sophia were overjoyed at the sight- help was on its way soon. They hugged each other and pointed up to the sky, as other neighbors came out to see what was going on. Everyone was shouting and jumping for joy, and Natasha, sensing their strange behavior as happiness, started barking and dancing around them. Richard picked Sophia up and swung her around as they both laughed and cried at the same time. He put her down, put his hands on her face, and said, "We did it, honey. We're gonna make it. I love you very much."

He kissed her, wrapped his arm around her slender waist, and walked her up their sidewalk and into their home, Natasha leading the way. As he crossed the threshold, a sobering thought crossed Richard's mind. This wasn't just the end; it was also a new and uncertain beginning.

## ABOUT THE AUTHOR

Douglas Thornblom is a retired Army Colonel and a graduate of the West Point class of 1966. After graduating from West Point, he earned his jump wings and his Ranger tab at Fort Benning, Georgia. During his 30-year Army career he served in combat in both Vietnam and El Salvador. He commanded an Airborne Infantry Rifle Company, a Mechanized Infantry Battalion, and a Basic Combat Training Battalion. He was also named a Senior Fellow at the State Department's Center for the Study of Foreign Affairs, and served three years as the Military Attaché to Spain.

He lives with his wife, Debbie, in Florida. They have two Siberian Huskies, Boris and Sasha.

And by the way, Debbie picked up the check on their first date.

If you enjoyed reading this book I would appreciate it if you would leave a review on Amazon. As a first time, and therefore unknown, author, ratings can make or break a first book. Just log onto the Amazon page for "Defending Sea Breezes":

http://www.amazon.com/dp/B01864XWFQ

Scroll down to "Customer Reviews," click on the block that says "Write a customer review" and compose your comments. Thanks!